THE MONSTER

IN THE MUDBALL

CHAPTER
ONE

Madalitso dragged a chair over to her wardrobe. It took almost all her strength. Shakily she climbed up onto it. Her legs were as thin as sticks. But her eyes blazed with fierce determination.

Her lips began to move. "Are you listening, Zilombo?" she whispered. "I know you can hear me in there."

She was talking quietly. There were only two things on top of her wardrobe. One was a battered cardboard suitcase—the one she'd brought with her, sixty years ago, when she came to England from Africa. The other was a ball of dried mud, slightly

1

bigger than a football and covered in dust and cobwebs.

"I have kept you shut up here for twenty years," said Madalitso. "That is a harsh punishment. But what else could we do after the terrible thing you did?"

Madalitso had a strange expression on her wrinkled face: anger and fear and sorrow all mixed up. Madalitso whispered on, wobbling on her chair. "I want you to know that this afternoon the inspector is coming. Yes, it's that time again! Time for her yearly visit, to make sure you can't escape. But there's no chance of that, is there? Not while I'm still alive."

Madalitso didn't notice a baby crawl in from the other room. The baby had spiky black hair. His face was shiny with drool.

He smeared the drool off his face with his chubby fist. Then he opened his fingers like a starfish, so the spit stretched between them in glistening strands. His face split into a big gummy grin, pleased at his own cleverness.

The baby looked up. He seemed to see Madalitso

for the first time. His eyes grew round with amazement. He held up his slimy hand to show her his drool cat's cradle.

"Goo!" he said.

For years Madalitso had kept her prisoner secret. And now someone was spying on her! She turned and thought, relieved, "It's only Smiler!" The baby's real name was Kai. But nobody ever called him that. Everyone always called him Smiler.

But now Madalitso's chair was rocking.

"Aiee!" she cried as she lost her balance. She reached out to grab the wardrobe for support. But that began swaying too. The dried-up mudball rolled to the front of the wardrobe, right onto Madalitso's desperately clutching fingers. She let go. At the same time, the chair slipped from beneath her. Madalitso tumbled to the floor.

A voice yelled from the other room. "Smiler, are you all right?"

Jin, Smiler's big brother, came bursting into the bedroom. He crashed into the bedside table, spun round and almost trampled Smiler. Then he saw

Madalitso, lying curled up, not moving, on the floor, and his mind scrambled immediately.

In a panic, he thought, *What do I do? What do I do?*

Then *Get Mum!* his brain screamed at him. Mum was Madalitso's friend. She was out in the backyard, emptying the kitchen bin.

"Mum!" bellowed Jin, loud enough for the whole street to hear. Smiler was the world's sunniest, giggliest baby. But now, scared silly by his big brother's panic, he made his mouth into a square red hole. He started shrieking like a car alarm, just to add to the din.

Jin's mum came racing in, still carrying the bin.

Her quick eyes took in the situation. She dropped the bin, then rummaged in her pocket for her mobile phone. She called an ambulance, then went to kneel beside Madalitso.

For years, Madalitso Lungu had been their next-door neighbor. Then she'd gotten old and frail and moved two streets away to this bungalow. Jin's mum often came round to do her shopping and housework for her. And when he wasn't busy working, Jin's dad came too, to do all her little odd jobs.

Mum knelt by Madalitso, muttering, "Where's that ambulance?"

Then they heard an ambulance siren wailing. Suddenly Madalitso's little bungalow was crowded with people. Paramedics took control. Gently they lifted Madalitso onto a stretcher. Jin squashed himself into a corner, out of the way, feeling helpless, useless. Smiler had stopped screeching. He was playing cat's cradle with his drool again. Then he got bored with that and crawled through the paramedics' legs to the other side of the bedroom where, unnoticed by anyone, the ball had rolled.

"Ooo," said Smiler, poking the mudball with his pudgy finger. As he crouched over it, his drool dribbled onto the dry mud, soaking through, making it sticky.

Suddenly Madalitso twitched. Jin felt dizzy with relief. She wasn't dead, after all! She stared woozily at Smiler. At first it seemed she didn't understand what she was seeing. Then her eyes grew wide with horror.

"No!" Madalitso shrieked, sitting bolt upright, as if she'd had an electric shock. She stretched out a trembling arm and pointed at Smiler, like a prophet of doom. "No! There is terrible danger!"

"Don't be afraid, Madalitso," soothed Mum. "These nice men are here to look after you."

"Danger," croaked Madalitso again, desperately. She strained to say something more. "Zilombo will escape! Tell the inspector!" But somehow her words came out in Chewa, the African language she spoke as a girl, so no one understood.

Madalitso fell back, exhausted, onto the stretcher. Her eyes closed and she lay quiet.

"Is she . . . d-dead?" stammered Jin, feeling sick and shivery inside.

Mum hissed, "Jin, don't ask such awful questions!"

"It's all right, sonny," said the paramedic. "Miss Lungu's just having a little rest." He reached out to give Jin a reassuring pat, as if he were a pet dog. Jin squirmed away. He hated people touching his head, mussing up his hair.

"What was Madalitso talking about?" puzzled Mum.

"What did she mean, 'danger'? I don't understand."

"Don't worry about it," said a paramedic. "She's had a nasty knock on the head. She probably doesn't know what she's saying."

The stretcher was wheeled outside with Jin's mum dashing anxiously beside it, her tiny shoes, embroidered with red dragons, slap-slapping on the pavement.

For a few minutes, Jin stayed hunched in a corner, his shocked brain trying to cope with what had just happened. Then he moved away from the wall and stumbled into the kitchen bin that mum had dropped. Jin hardly noticed. Because of his dyspraxia, things were always tripping him up, or breaking to bits in his hands.

Jin had clumsy child syndrome. It was no big deal and usually he forgot all about it. But it did sometimes make life more complicated. Today, for instance, he had his shoes on the wrong feet and his laces dangling because he couldn't tie them. No one minds that when you're a baby like Smiler. But when you're eleven, people notice.

He heard a chuckling from Smiler and went to see what he was up to.

"Where'd you get that?" Jin demanded. What was a big ball of mud doing in Madalitso's bedroom? Jin inspected it more closely. The ball seemed to have words carved on it. They were in a language Jin didn't understand. Not English. Not Chinese either.

"Don't!" Jin warned as Smiler licked the ball. Smiler was always tasting nasty things, like worms and other even more disgusting stuff that made Jin want to throw up.

"Stop it!" Jin ordered Smiler. "*Yuck!* Dirty!" Jin didn't know what it was. But it must belong to Madalitso or it wouldn't be here. Then he bent forward, startled. Something was happening to the ball. It was jiggling, like an egg about to hatch. Fine cracks, like a spider's web, spread out across its surface. One of the cracks began to widen.

Smiler thought it was a game. He chuckled, dribbled on the ball some more and made it even soggier. Then he put out a slimy hand to keep it still.

Suddenly Smiler cried out in alarm. He snatched

back his hand, as if from a fire. With ferocious swiftness, the ball had flipped itself over. Two big, bare feet thrust themselves out the bottom. Followed by a pair of scrawny ankles. One ankle had a bracelet on it: a bracelet made of many metal bottle tops threaded onto a leather thong.

Like a wild creature released from a trap, the ball of mud started bounding about, taking great kangaroo-like leaps, its ankle bracelet jingling.

Jin stared at it, astonished. Those bony toes had webs between them, like a duck. But apart from that, they looked horribly human. They seemed to be getting bigger as he watched. Then he noticed the toenails. They were yellow and horny. Some were long and sharp, like daggers; some curled into hooked claws.

What on earth is it? thought Jin.

Now the legs were visible up to the knee. They were chicken-thin. The skin was gray and scaly. But those legs were more powerful than they looked. They propelled the mudball, in one grotesque jangling spring, out the bedroom door. Then it pounded away on its great flat feet.

For a few seconds, Jin stood frozen with shock. But Smiler was hysterical. The world was bewildering enough for a baby. But now his ball had just sprouted legs and run away! He started wailing inconsolably. Outside the ambulance went nee-nawing off to the hospital with Madalitso inside. That made Jin's brain start working again.

Whatever that thing was, he had to get it back. He couldn't think why it should be important to Madalitso. But old people had some weird treasures. Grandma Sparks had a lucky cowboy hat she wore for bingo, even when she played it online.

Madalitso might think I took her ball! thought Jin wildly.

Part of him knew his fears were stupid. That Madalitso would never blame him. Anyway, who'd want to steal a mudball on legs?

Jin lurched out the front door. He bumped into Mum, coming back up the garden path.

"Did you see it?" Jin demanded. "Did you see which way it went?"

Mum stared at him. But she didn't seem to hear

him. She was too busy worrying about Madalitso.

"Hope she's all right," she muttered. "She's such a lovely old lady. But what was she thinking of, climbing up on that chair?"

But by then, Jin was running down the street.

"Catch you later, Mum," he bawled back over his shoulder.

CHAPTER
TWO

At first Jin thought he'd lost the mudball. He looked around frantically. Madalitso's bungalow was on a hill. You could see right over the city: tower blocks and metro trains and smoke from the factories, rising into a blue sky. A road sloped down to the wide gleaming river.

You could even see the sea today, a silver ribbon on the far horizon.

But Jin couldn't see a mudball pounding along the pavement. Just mums puffing up the hill pushing strollers. And kids racing bikes down it at breakneck speed.

Jin ran down the road a bit.

I've lost it, he thought.

Then suddenly he heard a faint jingle off to his right. This was the old part of the city. Steps and cobbled alleyways were everywhere, tucked between buildings, often only narrow enough for just one person. And there was the mudball, like some weird beast half-hatched from its shell, sneaking down a steep flight of stone steps.

For a few seconds Jin watched its creepy descent. It was feeling its way. Its long bony toes, with their talon nails, carefully gripped the edge of each step. It stretched out a spidery leg, feeling about, before it planted a webbed foot on the next. It couldn't be a robot, could it? Some kind of electronic gizmo?

Every few seconds, the mudball tilted upward, like a dog sniffing the air. But how could it do that? It had no nose, no facial features at all. The only things on that blank mud sphere were a few cracks and those mysterious carved words.

"Hey, wait!" yelled Jin, without thinking.

He saw the mudball pause, its legs frozen in

mid-creep. And the ball turned round, like some blind, faceless head. It swiveled in Jin's direction, as if it could hear him.

Jin shivered. He felt an icy prickling at the back of his neck.

"It's like it's alive," he whispered.

But the ball had taken off again. It seemed to know exactly where it was going.

Jin plunged down the steps after it, his legs wobbling, his arms whirling like windmills to keep his balance.

"Concentrate!" he warned himself through gritted teeth. If he concentrated he usually, despite his clumsiness, could force his disobedient limbs to behave. "Hey! I'm catching up with it!" he congratulated himself.

But now the mudball had disappeared. As Jin clattered to the bottom of the stone steps he was just in time to see it leap across the road with a mighty spring. A driver stopped, brakes squealing, as it sailed past his windscreen, its webbed feet tucked beneath it like a flying duck. The driver peered out, shook a furious fist at Jin, as if he thought he'd thrown it.

"Nothing to do with me!" mouthed Jin, throwing his arms wide and giving a big, helpless shrug.

He stumbled after the mudball into the gloomy alley. The alley smelled dank and reedy. That's because at the end of it was the Oozeburn, a muddy tidal stream that flowed into the big river. Jin knew the Oozeburn well because his Granny and Grandad Tang lived down there. But why should the mudball be heading in that direction? The Oozeburn was in a run-down part of the city. The main river was lined with posh buildings and apartments, but there was nothing on the Oozeburn's banks except weedy wastelands and derelict, boarded-up buildings.

But Jin didn't have time to wonder about that. He didn't want to lose sight of the mudball. Not after he'd followed it this far. And, besides getting it back for Madalitso, he was madly curious too. He wanted a closer look. Wanted to find out what that robot, that creature, that *thing*, really was.

"I've never seen anything like it in my whole life!" marveled Jin.

He'd forgotten that prickle of fear he felt before. The *thing* was definitely bizarre. Ghoulish, even. *But basically,* he reassured himself, *it's just a ball of mud with big flat feet. I mean, how dangerous could that be?*

"Ouch!" Jin crashed into a smelly old trash can that spilled moldy pizza and chewed chicken wings over his shoes. "That's what you get for not concentrating," he told himself sternly. The alley was crowded with stinking bins, like an obstacle course. Not the best place for a chase. He groaned. "I've lost it again!" He smacked his hand off his forehead in exasperation. Then gave a surprised gasp.

There was the mudball, moving out of the shadows and into the open.

But then a harsh squawk came from overhead. It was an enormous seagull. It had spied the mudball from a rooftop, thinking it was something tasty.

It came flapping down onto a trash bin and folded its great white wings.

The mudball turned slightly on its wiry chicken legs, like it knew the gull was there. But it didn't seem bothered.

Why doesn't it run? thought Jin.

Maybe it didn't know about the city's seagulls. Those gulls were savage. They had claws like velociraptors. And beaks that could snap a pigeon's neck. They snatched burgers and ice cream cones from kids. They dive-bombed bald guys and raked at their heads, drawing blood.

And this wasn't just any old gull. It was a monster bird. It had a brutal, hooked beak and tiny sharklike eyes.

A gull this big could swoop off with your pet Chihuahua. A gull this big couldn't just kill a pigeon. It could rip it wide open, shake it inside out, and gobble its guts.

The great gull fluttered down from the bin, almost lazily, as if it didn't anticipate any trouble from this strange, hopping, froglike creature. Maybe, like it did with pigeons, it planned to rip it open and gobble up what was inside.

It was right next to the mudball now. The mudball wasn't moving. It had hidden its feet beneath it, like a broody hen. The gull strutted around it, gave an experimental stab with its beak . . .

Then Jin heard a noise. It was a sudden rattle. Short, harsh, and chilling, like clashing spears. It was the mudball's bottle-top ankle bracelet.

The gull stabbed again.

Again, the mudball stamped its foot. That menacing rattle sounded once, twice, like a war cry.

Then, lightning quick, the mudball attacked. A bony foot shot out sideways like a kickboxer. Those long toes seized the gull round its neck with a gorilla-like grip. The gull screeched once. Then the foot slammed the bird onto its back, where it squirmed frantically, beating great white wings like a fallen angel. The mudball's toes, with their yellow talon nails, tightened.

"It's strangling the gull!" gasped Jin.

The mudball tilted upward again, like a dog sniffing a scent on the breeze. Abruptly it stopped throttling the gull and sprang away. As if it had more urgent things to do.

The freed bird fluttered woozily to its feet. Then it took off, burst out of the alley in a blizzard of white feathers and went screeching off into the blue sky. It obviously wanted to get as far away from its attacker as it could.

Jin could hardly believe what he'd just seen. His mouth was still hanging open in amazement. The mudball was bounding to the end of the alley, as if nothing had happened.

Jin, more wary now, followed it, keeping a safe distance.

CHAPTER
THREE

The mudball was heading straight for the Oozeburn, as if drawn by a magnet.

Most of Jin's attention was on keeping up, and not crashing into anything. But what did flash through his mind was: *That's peculiar.* Most city dwellers didn't know the Oozeburn existed. But Grandad and Grandma Tang lived there because they needed a big space to run their business. And, besides, they were fond of the weedy, neglected backwater.

Jin followed the mudball down some slimy stone steps. At the bottom was the towpath that ran alongside the canal. The path was choked by tall purple weeds and brambles.

A bramble looped itself round his leg, tried to trip him up. Then another snared him. Jin wasn't surprised. Things often seemed to gang up on him. Patiently he stooped to untangle the spiky branches.

"Ow!" he protested as spines stabbed his hand. "Where's that mudball gone now?" he muttered, licking the blood off his fingers.

He gazed up and down the towpath, looking for it. Metro trains rattled by overhead on high railway bridges. Gleaming office blocks and posh flats were being built all around. But down here, right in the city center, was a forgotten world.

This stretch of the Oozeburn flowed through a deep, brick-lined channel that ran between derelict factories, some many stories high. The buildings dated back to Victorian times. Everything here was a relic from the city's industrial past. You could almost feel the ghosts.

There were big iron rings on the towpath where barges had once been moored. Rusty iron ladders went down the slimy brick walls, right to the water.

Only there was no water now at the bottom of the deep channel. Because the tide was out, there was just greasy mud, with old, wrecked boats sticking up like rotten teeth and ratty-looking ducks draggling about among dumped shopping carts.

But there was no mudball, kangarooing along on big, bony feet that had casually almost choked that seagull to death.

Jin listened for its ankle bracelet—those jangling bottle tops. But the only rattle he heard was a metro train, speeding way overhead.

"Think I'm going mad," murmured Jin, staring down from the towpath at the muddy riverbed. In a minute, maybe he'd wake up, find it was all a bad dream.

"Hi, Bro," came a cool, sardonic voice.

Jin whirled round. It was his big sister Frankie, lounging along the towpath toward him. Frankie was slight, bird-boned like Mum and Grandma Tang. But she'd inherited their dad's height. She looked, as usual, like a fairy at a funeral. Except for those thick woolly black tights and clomping biker boots.

Frankie bought party frocks from charity shops. Frothy, fancy frocks with big skirts, dripping with lace and net layers and frills and sequins. But she always dyed them deepest black. She painted her fingernails and toenails black to match.

"You a Goth?" Jin had once asked her.

"I'm not anything!" Frankie had fumed, insulted. "I'm me, right? Just me. Frankie."

"What are you doing here?" Jin asked her. All the time, his eyes kept sliding around, searching for the mudball. He opened his mouth to ask Frankie about it, then closed it again. He couldn't think of the right words. *She'll think I'm pulling her leg, being cheeky or something*, he thought. And Frankie wasn't the kind of girl you were cheeky to. Not if you wanted to live.

Meanwhile Frankie was saying, "I'm going to see Grandad and Granny Tang. I had a row with Mum this morning."

"You been dyeing your frocks in the bath again?" sighed Jin. "You been doing graffiti?"

"I always do graffiti." Frankie grinned.

That was true. Jin had seen Frankie's tag all over the city.

"You been keeping your spray cans under your bed again?" asked Jin.

Dad always went mental when Frankie did that. He said it was really dangerous.

"Anyhoo, Frankie," said Jin, his eyes flickering around, taking in the crumbling buildings, weedy towpath, and the greasy riverbed. "I'm looking for something. And I know this sounds really weird, but have you seen—?"

Suddenly a high-pitched wail of distress came from the building behind them. Most of its windows were boarded over. Except for its very top windows five stories up. And that's where the voice came from. *"Aiiii!"* Another wail came drifting down. "What will become of us?"

"Granny Tang!" said Frankie, her eyes shooting upward to those high windows.

She and Jin went racing into the building and made for the stairs.

Despite her clumsy boots, Frankie went streaking upward like an arrow, her long black hair whipping around her face. Jin clattered after her, trying not to trip. Their footsteps echoed, loud and eerie. The old Victorian building was as bare and freezing as an empty fridge. It had been a factory once, making pottery. Then it had been turned into flats. But over the years, it had become run-down. All the other tenants had moved out. Now Granny and Grandad Tang were the only people left.

Frankie crashed, breathless, into their grand-parents' flat with Jin not far behind. The Tangs made dragons for Chinese New Year celebrations. The dragons' wolflike heads, made out of bamboo and paper and painted in bright colors, were all over the place. They looked fantastic, half comical and half ferocious. They had goggling eyes like Ping-Pong balls, tufty eyebrows, and sharp white fangs in bloodred, gaping mouths.

"What's up, Gran?" gasped Frankie.

Gran was a tiny lady in a thick, padded jacket. Her peachy skin had gone gray with shock. Grandad Tang stood by. Even his usually serene face looked troubled.

Frantic thoughts whirled through Jin's mind. They

hadn't seen the mudball, had they? That was enough to give anyone a funny turn.

"You haven't seen it, have you?" gabbled Jin, jigging about in a panic. "This sort of mudball thing, with legs and an ankle bracelet made out of bottle tops?"

Frankie shot Jin a killer glare. "What are you on about?" she snapped.

But the Tangs' distress was nothing to do with the mudball.

"This just came in the post," said Gran, holding out an official-looking letter with trembling fingers.

Jin took some deep breaths, forced himself to shut up, calm down, and stop flapping his hands. He waited for Gran to explain some more. But it was Grandad who took up the story.

"This letter says that we have to leave our home. That they are going to demolish this building. And build executive apartments."

"No way, Grandad!" protested Frankie, outraged.

"Where shall we go?" wailed Grandma Tang. "How can we run our dragon business?"

Tang dragons were famous. Orders came from Chinese communities all over the country. Propped by the window, on two long bamboo poles, was a splendid one they'd just finished. At three meters long he was one of their smallest dragons. Some dragons were so long they needed twenty people to work them. It would only take two people to carry this one, to raise and lower him on those long poles, make him seem to dance to the wild music of drums and gongs and cymbals. His fierce dragon head was crimson, his goggly eyes were gold. His long, snaky body, made out of glittering fabric draped over bamboo hoops, was golden too. He had a crimson crest running down his spine. And all over him were decorations that would shake and glitter as he danced: silver fringes and mirrors and golden disks.

"But, Grandma, they can't just chuck you out!" Frankie was raving. "You've got rights! Who do they think they are? I'm going to call Mum," she decided, forgetting about the row she and Mum had had that morning. "Wait until Mum hears about this! She'll go ballistic!"

While Frankie paced around like a tiger, jabbing at her mobile, trying to reach Mum, Jin found himself sidling toward the windows. A metro train rushed by and rattled the glass. The high railway bridge spanned the main river and the Oozeburn, then soared right over the factory roof, just missing its chimneys.

Jin stared down at the Oozeburn, far below. Beside him, the dancing dragon seemed to stare too, with its goggly golden eyes.

Suddenly, on the smooth, glossy mud of the streambed, a grotesque shadow fell. The afternoon sun stretched it out, made its legs long and spindly.

"The mudball!" Jin hissed, feeling a creeping chill. It must be hiding somewhere on the towpath. "Sorry, things to do," he called over his shoulder as he galloped toward the stairs.

Behind him, no one noticed him go. Frankie was jabbering into her mobile. Grandma Tang had her head bent over that dreadful letter, reading it again, mouthing the words in disbelief. Grandad Tang stood behind her, patting her shoulders, trying to comfort her.

"Don't worry," he was saying. "We'll set up our business somewhere else. We've survived plenty worse things than this."

Jin went hurtling downstairs, missing steps, bouncing off walls. But somehow he managed not to trip and break his neck. He burst out into the sunshine. The Oozeburn was peaceful in the afternoon heat. Bees were buzzing along the towpath among the dusty weeds.

Jin's eyes darted round. He felt a sick fluttering in the pit of his stomach. Things had changed since he'd set out in pursuit of the mudball. He'd felt bewildered then and wondered, *What on earth is it?* But he hadn't felt scared. It had even been comical, watching it hopping along. But then he'd watched it almost kill the gull. And things had suddenly taken a very sinister turn.

"Think before you do things," Mum had often warned Jin. "Think of the risks. If you go rushing in recklessly, you are more likely than other kids to have accidents."

And Jin *was* cautious, most of the time. But sometimes he got bored of calculating risks. Sometimes, he just let his wild, impulsive side take over. He just couldn't help himself.

So he went rushing in recklessly, whipping at the weeds with a piece of old rope he found on the towpath, trying to flush the mudball into the open.

He saw something scuttling, thought, *I've found it!*

But it was only a rat. It skipped across the towpath and leaped into the channel. When Jin looked down, the rat hadn't landed on the riverbed. On the far side of the Oozeburn, set into the brick wall, was a round iron grid, the size of a tractor wheel. The rat was clinging to that. With a whisk of its tail it squeezed through the grid. Behind the grid was a sewage pipe that had once emptied into the Oozeburn. The sewage pipe wasn't used anymore. But it went for miles under the city, or so people said.

Jin slumped down on the towpath, exhausted.

Then caution began to creep in. "What were you going to do if you'd found it?" he asked himself. The mudball could run faster than him. And it could certainly defend itself. It wouldn't just stand still quietly and let him catch it.

Jin sighed deeply. He often had days when he thought the world was crazy. But this day had been the freakiest day in his whole life, so far.

He decided to give up the search.

Better go back, he thought. *Back to Mum and Smiler.* Mum would be wondering where he'd gotten to.

He thought, briefly, of going back into the factory, to find out how Granny and Grandad Tang were coping. But he just couldn't face any more drama, not at the moment. He'd leave that particular crisis to Frankie. He'd had enough stress, what with Madalitso and the mudball. Why did she keep such a dangerous thing in her house? It couldn't be some kind of pet, could it? Some kind of weird exotic creature?

"Naaah," he told himself, shaking his head. He was a city kid—he didn't know much about animals. But who'd be mad enough to keep something so wild and savage as a pet?

Jin tried to imagine putting the mudball on a lead like a tame pooch, taking it to the park for walkies.

Teaching it to fetch sticks, to sit up and beg for doggy treats.

"Naaah." Jin shook his head again. "Don't be ridiculous."

Whatever that thing was, it wasn't anyone's pet. You'd have to keep it in a cage behind metal bars. *And even then,* Jin thought, shivering, *I wouldn't feel safe.* He could imagine it prizing apart the strongest bars with those powerful toes, squeezing through.

So why had Madalitso kept it on top of her wardrobe? Not even locked up? Like some kind of harmless, dusty old ornament?

Jin frowned. Questions collided in his brain like bumper cars. Had the mudball finished growing? Was any more of it going to appear, apart from those legs and feet?

Jin crammed his hands over his ears. "Just shut up!" he ordered his clamoring brain. "You're driving me crazy!"

He plodded off, retracing his steps.

Behind him, all seemed quiet along the Oozeburn. There was no one to see what happened next.

A long, taloned foot crept out of the spiny brambles, the toes feeling around, exploring. Then another. Then the whole mudball burst out and hopped to the edge of the towpath. About two meters below was the Oozeburn. There was still no water in the channel, just mud and stones, slippery with green slime.

But the mudball raised itself on its scaly legs, tilted upward. It could smell the tide coming in.

With one great froggy leap, it sprang down to the riverbed. It sank immediately in the sloppy mud, down, down, until, with a sucking sound like a sink plunger, the mud closed over the ball.

Minutes passed. A metro train clattered by, high above, and disappeared over the flat roof of the factory where Jin's grandparents lived.

The rat came squeezing back through the grid that covered the sewage pipe. It sprang down to the riverbed. It went snuffling over the stones, looking for crabs. It skittered here and there across the mud, not heavy enough to sink, leaving a scribble of tiny paw prints.

Suddenly a clawed foot shot out of the mud, snatched the rat round its middle, and dragged it down. The rat was so surprised at being ambushed it didn't even have time to squeak.

With its next meal grasped in one foot, the mudball stayed quietly hidden. It had been waiting for years and years. But it wouldn't be long now. It could feel vibrations through the mud. The tide was turning. The sea was flooding into the big main river. Soon even scummy little creeks, like the Oozeburn, would fill with water. Then, at last, the mudball's long imprisonment would be over.

Meanwhile Jin, retracing his route, had reached the alleyway crammed with trash cans.

He still had the faint, desperate hope that the mudball was some kind of hallucination. That his mind had been playing tricks. But when he trudged back up the alley steps, that hope shriveled and died. The mudball was real, all right. Here was the exact place where it had attacked the gull. White feathers were still scattered around. And here, in some spilled sawdust, was a clear print of one weird, webbed foot.

Jin shuddered. You could even see its talons.

Jin hurried out of the dark alley, into the bright, sunlit street. It was a huge relief to see normal things happening: traffic roaring by, kids riding bikes, mums pushing strollers.

He decided to head first for Madalitso's bungalow. Mum and Smiler might still be there. If not, they'd be at home. Unless Mum had gone to the hospital to see how Madalitso was doing.

Jin could have checked if he'd had a mobile phone. But Mum had put her foot down. "No more mobiles," she had said. "It's costing me a fortune!"

"Anyhoo," said Jin, "it's not my fault I keep breaking them. I've got clumsy child syndrome, haven't I?"

"You can't use that as an excuse," Mum had answered. "You left the last one on the bus!"

Jin battered on the door of Madalitso's bungalow. There was no sign of Mum or Smiler inside. But he battered on the door a bit more, then rattled the door handle furiously.

A calm voice said behind him, "Do you want to make that house fall down?"

CHAPTER
FOUR

Jin spun round, startled. A tall, majestic lady stood on the pavement, watching him. She had an eye patch over one eye. Where on earth had she sprung from?

The lady opened the gate and marched up Madalitso's garden path. She seized Jin's hand and shook it. "Good afternoon," she greeted him.

"Excuse me," stammered Jin as his arm was pumped up and down in her powerful grip. "Excuse me, but who—who are you?"

"I am the inspector, of course," she told him. "Madalitso is expecting me."

Jin stared at her, his eyes popping. He'd seen

inspectors before, in his school. But they mostly sneaked around silently, wearing gray suits, blending into the background. They said things like, "Pretend I'm not here."

This inspector was nothing at all like that. Everything about her shrieked, "I have arrived!"

She'd burst like a firework display into this quiet little cul de sac of gray, pebble-dashed bungalows. She had a wrap wound into a high crown around her head. Her head wrap and skirt were the same pattern—sizzling-hot red, flaming orange, and scorching yellow zigzags.

She was over six feet tall, Jin guessed, with high cheekbones and a proud upward tilt to her chin. One eye was covered by the patch. But the other was deep amber. She seemed to Jin's astonished gaze like a cross between a warrior queen and a pirate.

"You don't look like an inspector," he babbled.

The inspector looked down at him sternly, and Jin thought, *Have I said something rude?*

But then a smile briefly softened the sharp angles of her face.

"In fact, I am the chief inspector," she informed

Jin. "From the Risk Assessment Agency for Ancient Artifacts."

"From what?" said Jin.

"That is RAAAA, for short."

"RAAAAA?" repeated Jin, looking bewildered.

"Not bad," said the inspector. "But I think you have got one too many *a*'s there. Anyway, my name is A. J. Zauyamakanda."

Jin took a wild stab at that: "A. J. Zauyamakararanda?"

"Now you have got far too many *a*'s," said the inspector, her eye flashing in disapproval. "Do children in this country have a problem with that letter?"

"Er, no." Jin shook his head, more flustered than ever. "I don't know. I never thought about it!" He hoped he didn't have a problem with *a*'s. He had enough things to worry about without adding that to the list.

"You had better call me Mizz Z," said the inspector in condescending tones.

"Miss Z?" repeated Jin.

"Actually, that is with three *z*'s," Mizz Z informed

him. "I happen to particularly like the letter z," she added mysteriously.

"You like the letter z?" echoed Jin, his brain spinning.

"Yes, and what is wrong with that?" asked Mizz Z. "Don't say you have problems with the last letter of the alphabet as well as the first!"

Jin opened his mouth to answer. But, this time, nothing at all came out except, "Errr, errr . . ."

"So exactly where is Madalitso?" Mizz Z demanded briskly.

Jin tried to get his thoughts together and say something sensible. "She's in the hospital," he told the inspector. "She fell off a chair and bashed her head."

"That is very bad news," said Mizz Z. "Is she dead?"

"No," said Jin, startled by Mizz Z's directness. Mum had told him off for asking the paramedic that question. But Mizz Z obviously didn't think there was anything wrong with it. "And the ambulance guy said she wasn't going to die," Jin added.

"That is something good at least," declared Mizz Z. She lowered herself from her great height and squatted down on her heels. "Sit here," she ordered Jin, pointing at the front doorstep. Jin sat on the step facing her. Her amber eye stared into his. "I am going to ask you a very important question," said Mizz Z. "When Madalitso went into the hospital, did she take anything with her? An ancient artifact of any kind?"

"I don't think so," said Jin, shaking his head.

"Then the artifact I need to inspect must still be inside her house," said Mizz Z.

"Look," admitted Jin, "I'm a bit confused about this 'artifact' thing."

"Is that because it starts with an *a*?" asked Mizz Z, with a pitying shake of her head.

Jin clenched his fists in frustration. "I told you, I don't have a problem with *a*'s! My name's Jin Aaron Sparks and—"

"Aaron?" interrupted Mizz Z. "Where did that name come from?"

"It's from my dad," Jin explained hurriedly. "His name's Aaron Sparks."

"Ah, I see," said Mizz Z.

"Anyway," Jin rushed on, "like I was saying, my name's got three *a*'s in it! I've had that name my whole life and I've never had a problem with it! Or with *z*'s either, by the way!"

"Dear me," said Mizz Z calmly. "Kids in this country are extremely touchy!"

"It's just," said Jin, gnashing his teeth, "that I'm not sure what an ancient artifact is, exactly."

Mizz Z unslung her backpack from her shoulders. She unzipped it and pulled out a laptop. The bronze bracelets on her arm clashed as she moved.

"I will show you," she said. She powered up the laptop and hit a flurry of keys. "Here are just a few ancient artifacts."

Pictures of fearsome masks, golden coins, spears, statues, and beautiful embroidered kimonos flashed across the screen.

"But I must admit," said Mizz Z, "that the artifact in this case is rather unusual. It's a ball made out of mud, which has certain words carved all over it."

Jin felt his guts clench tightly. He tried to speak,

but the words stuck in his throat like stones.

Mizz Z's eye narrowed. "So you know of this artifact?" she asked sharply, as if she could read his mind.

Jin nodded dumbly.

"And it is inside the bungalow? On top of Madalitso's wardrobe? Where I ordered it should be kept, for safety?"

Still dumb, Jin shook his head. Then he managed to splutter, "No, it escaped."

"Escaped?" repeated Mizz Z, fixing him with a fiery eye.

"It grew legs," babbled Jin. "Its feet were half-frog, half-human and it nearly killed a seagull. Strangled it with its feet, and it had yellow toenails, like sharp claws, and this ankle bracelet that it kept, like, *rattling*, made out of bottle tops!"

He waited for Mizz Z to hoot with scornful laughter.

But instead she said, in a mildly irritated voice, "That is a bit of a nuisance."

Jin's mouth fell open. "You believe me?"

Mizz Z said, "Why, you are not lying, are you?"

"Well, no, I just thought . . ."

But Mizz Z was already saying, "It ran toward the river, didn't it?"

This time Jin's mouth sagged open so far that, before he could speak again, he had to take his chin in his hand and slam it shut. At last he stuttered, amazed, "How'd you know that?"

Mizz Z gave an impatient shrug. "Because I know about this mudball. I know its habits. Trust me, I have great experience in these matters." She hit some more keys, then went quiet for a moment, staring at the screen. "Ah, that is excellent," she said.

"What's excellent?" Jin couldn't stop himself asking.

"I am a football coach in my spare time," explained Mizz Z, "back home, in my country. And I was just checking the website of my girls' football team, the Lakeside Queens. They have won again!"

"Congratulations!" said Jin automatically. "You must be over the moon!"

"But back to business," said Mizz Z, stashing away her laptop. "I am on a tight schedule. I have many artifacts to inspect in your city. Now show me this river where the mudball went." She rose in one graceful movement. "Did the mudball get wet in some way?" she enquired.

"Er, yeah," admitted Jin. "My baby brother, Smiler, drooled on it."

Mizz Z pursed her lips. "It must have been enough to start off the hatching-out process. Did you not read the warnings carved all over the ball: 'Never, ever, get this ball wet! Or you will regret it!'"

"But weren't they in some kind of foreign language?" asked Jin.

"Yes," said Mizz Z. "Chewa, actually. One of the many languages in my country. Which is Malawi, which is in Africa, of course. But I hear you English kids do not learn foreign languages."

"I'm not just English," Jin pointed out. "I'm half English and half Chinese."

"So do you speak Mandarin?"

"Not very well," admitted Jin. "My Mum does and my Granny and Grandad Tang. But, like I said, I'm only half Chinese."

"That is no excuse," said Mizz Z sternly. "A half-Chinese boy should still speak Mandarin."

Jin opened his mouth to protest, "I know a few words!"

"And what about Chewa," added Mizz Z. "Why do you not speak that?"

Jin closed his mouth again. How could you argue with a crazy opinion like that? It was beyond ridiculous! Why should he know Chewa? He'd never even heard of it until just now!

But Mizz Z seemed to think it was perfectly reasonable. She seized her bag. "Let us get going," she commanded Jin. "Or I shall be late for my next inspection. Which way?"

"To the main road," said Jin. "Then left."

"Wait," said Mizz Z suddenly. She slid a mobile phone out of the side pocket of her backpack. "I suppose I had better alert the head office of RAAAA to this little setback."

Jin noticed, jealously, that Mizz Z had a really cool mobile. "You phoning Africa?" he asked her.

But Mizz Z was busy listening to her mobile. "Why

do they not answer?" she snapped impatiently, flashing her single eye. She listened again, then shook her head. "Still no answer! They must be out to lunch," she announced briskly, putting her mobile away.

She went marching off, her backpack bouncing on her shoulders.

"Oh, and by the way," Mizz Z flung back, over her shoulder. "That ankle bracelet you spoke of—the one the mudball was wearing. Those bottle tops were from Fanta bottles. It is a fizzy orange drink. Do you have it in this country?"

Jin didn't answer. He was too busy racing after her, willing himself not to trip or his legs to get tangled up. You certainly couldn't lose Mizz Z in a crowd. She was a tall woman. But her high head wrap and the thick soles of her flip-flops made her even loftier. She towered over everyone else in the busy street. Her bright clothes, her eye patch, and her stately manner drew many stares.

"Wow, is she a celebrity?" called a girl. "A model or a singer or something?"

"She's the chief inspector!" gasped Jin as he hurtled by. "And a football coach in her spare time!"

Finally he caught up with Mizz Z. "Down this alley," he panted. "It's a shortcut to the Oozeburn."

Mizz Z raised her head, sniffed the air. "I smell the sea," she said. "Is the tide out, or in?"

"It's coming in," said Jin.

"A pity," declared Mizz Z coolly. "That might make my job a tiny bit trickier."

CHAPTER
FIVE

Even then Mizz Z didn't seem much alarmed. She didn't quicken her pace. As if this runaway mudball was just a minor inconvenience. And Jin was reassured by her mighty confidence. He didn't feel scared now that she was with him.

But he felt just as mixed up as before. There were so many things he wanted to know. Like why she was wearing an eye patch. So he asked her.

"Why are you wearing that eye patch?"

But she didn't seem to hear him. Or she didn't want to answer.

So instead he said: "This agency that you're the inspector for?"

"I am chief inspector," Mizz Z reminded him.

"OK, chief inspector. Anyhoo, this agency—"

"RAAAA?" interrupted Mizz Z, with a spine-tingling, wolflike snarl.

"Yeah," shuddered Jin. "Anyhoo . . ."

"What is this word 'anyhoo'?" demanded Mizz Z.

"It's just the way I say 'anyhow,'" Jin explained impatiently.

"Why do you not say the word correctly?" enquired Mizz Z.

"Look, I don't know. It's just what I always say. It's not important, is it?" Jin felt his teeth clenching again with frustration. He'd thought his big sister Frankie was an awkward customer. But she was a pussycat compared to Mizz Z.

"Anyhoo," Jin continued doggedly. "I mean, *anyhow*, what does your agency *do*, exactly?"

Mizz Z paused by a trash can. She stared at Jin down her nose.

"I shall try to keep it simple," she said. "Here goes. Every year, I come to your country. I inspect ancient artifacts. These artifacts are kept all over the place—in museums, in dusty attics, even on the tops of wardrobes. I make sure they are being kept safely. That there is no risk."

"Risk?" repeated Jin, bewildered. "What kind of risk? Are these ancient artifacts all dangerous or something, like the mudball?"

"If you think the mudball is dangerous now, you have seen nothing yet," was Mizz Z's muttered reply.

"But do the owners of these things *know* they're dangerous?" Jin persisted.

Mizz Z cast Jin an approving glance. Maybe this boy was smarter than he looked. He was asking her some very shrewd questions. They deserved straight answers. But should she tell him the truth, what her job really involved? *Why not?* Mizz Z decided. *Since he knows so much already.*

And anyway, he was only some random child. What harm was there in him knowing? No one would believe him if he told anybody.

"Madalitso knew her artifact might be dangerous," Mizz Z told Jin. "But she was an exception. Most owners of the things I inspect have no idea. They don't know what power is hanging on their walls, or stored, forgotten, in trunks in their attics."

"Don't you tell them?" asked Jin.

"Of course not," said Mizz Z with a scathing look. "Why scare people if you don't need to? Besides, many owners don't even know I have visited. I do many of my inspections under cover of darkness."

"Wow!" said Jin, impressed. "What, you mean you sneak into places? Like a secret agent or something?"

"A chief inspector does not *sneak* anywhere," said Mizz Z loftily. "In any case, most ancient artifacts are perfectly harmless. Only a few have hidden powers. But even with them, that power is only released if the right conditions occur."

"What, like the mudball getting wet?" asked Jin.

Again, Mizz Z nodded. "Exactly right," she said. "I must say you are quite quick on the uptake. I am surprised, actually, that you believe it so easily—that there can be hidden power in objects."

"Course I believe it," said Jin fervently. He thought of all the times that the most ordinary things—like trash cans, bramble bushes, milk cartons—could turn treacherous. Some days even his shoelaces seemed to conspire against him. Things would lie in wait to ambush him, trip him up, confuse him. He was the last kid to underestimate the hidden power of objects. "It's like they come alive," he said in an awed whisper. "And cause you loads of trouble."

Mizz Z nodded in agreement. "I know the feeling," she said.

Jin thought, *She's speaking my language! She understands!* He asked her eagerly, "Have you got dyspraxia too?"

"What is that?" asked Mizz Z. "I have never heard of it."

"Never mind," mumbled Jin. "It's not important."

Mizz Z's face softened. She looked at Jin with new respect. "You are a very *wise* child, it seems to me," she said.

Jin stared at her. Was he hearing right? He'd been called lots of things in his life but never, ever, *wise*.

"What did you say your name was again?" asked Mizz Z, as if she'd suddenly thought his name was worth remembering.

"Jin. Jin Aaron Sparks," he told her.

"Well, Jin Aaron Sparks," said Mizz Z. "I believe we can work together. I may need a guide to this city. Someone who knows its secret places."

Me, a guide? thought Jin, suddenly feeling panicky. He had no sense of direction. He sometimes got lost in supermarkets. Countless times, he'd mistimed his exit and gotten stuck in a metro train's sliding doors.

"My big sister Frankie knows this city better than anyone," he tried to convince Mizz Z. "She knows all its secret places. She's done graffiti in most of them! You need Frankie for a guide, not me."

But Mizz Z, it seemed, was too far away to hear him. "Do we go this way?" she called back.

"Wait," shouted Jin. "There's something else I want to ask you!" Panting, he caught up with her. "These hidden powers you talked about, in the artifacts you inspect. Well, what powers has the mudball got?"

When Jin asked about the mudball's powers, he saw Mizz Z's hand sneak up to touch her black eye patch, as if that had something to do with it. To his surprise, her eye suddenly took on a haunted look.

But then she shook herself and seemed to recover.

She strode off, proud and dignified as before, her car-tire shoes thwacking the cobbles.

"There is no time now to tell you the mudball's story," she called back to Jin. "That must wait until later."

When they got down to the Oozeburn, instead of mud and stones, there was a little river flowing at the bottom of the channel. They stared down at it from the towpath. Gray scummy water slapped against the brick walls. Scruffy ducks paddled about, quacking happily.

Frankie was on the towpath, spray painting her tag on the walls of the old factory. It only took her a few swooping squirts. And there was a red Chinese dragon, with flames shooting out of its mouth in the shape of a spiky F.

"Hmmmm, that is quite clever," said Mizz Z.

Frankie whirled round, the ribbons on her black party frock whipping about her like tentacles. She wasn't used to being caught in the act. The places where she sprayed her tag—in derelict parts of the city, on boarded-up empty buildings, weedy rubble-strewn wastelands—were almost always lonely and deserted.

She glared at the intruder, checking her out—from her headgear, with its sizzling colors, to her backpack and flip-flops. Frankie was used to being the tallest among her friends. But Mizz Z towered over her.

Frankie turned to Jin. "Who's she?" she demanded.

"Excuse me, but is not spraying dragons everywhere illegal?" commented Mizz Z.

Frankie's eyes immediately blazed defiance. She got enough of that kind of talk from Mum. This stranger should mind her own business! Frankie sprayed her answer on the wall in a few quick, furious blasts. "SO WHAT?" it said, in huge, spiky red capitals.

"Who *is* she?" she asked Jin again, deliberately turning her back on Mizz Z, ignoring her. "What's she doing here?" She tapped her black glossy nails on her paint can while she waited for Jin's answer. But Mizz Z spoke up for herself.

"*She* is the cat's mother," she informed Frankie mildly.

Frankie whisked round, scowling. Jin thought,

Oh no! Frankie's going to say something really rude!
So he leaped in first. "Frankie, this is A. J. Zauya . . .
A. J. Zauya . . ." he stammered.

Mizz Z raised her eyebrows.

"Just call her Mizz Z," said Jin, with one of his
wide, helpless shrugs. "That's with three *z*'s," he
added. "She's a football coach in her spare time. By
the way, what did the Lakeside Queens win by?" he
asked Mizz Z.

"Five–nil," Mizz Z told him, with more than a hint
of pride. "They are well on their way to becoming
schoolgirl league champions."

"Five–nil!" marveled Jin. "They stormed it!"

"You are right to be impressed," said Mizz Z. "It
was a tough match. At halftime, soldier ants invaded
the pitch . . ."

"Soldier ants?" asked Jin, puzzled.

"They eat flesh," Mizz Z informed him. "They can
strip a small deer to its skeleton in six minutes."

As she listened to this weird conversation, Frankie's
scowl grew even stormier. She didn't have a clue
what they were talking about. And she didn't like

being ignored. "I am still here, you know," she protested.

Suddenly Mizz Z swung round and gave Frankie her full attention. Even Frankie quailed beneath that fierce, burning gaze. But when Mizz Z spoke, her voice was surprisingly warm and friendly.

"I like your style," she told Frankie. "It is spot-on. You shop in charity shops, then customize. Am I right? Eco-friendly. And creative!"

Frankie tried to look indifferent to Mizz Z's praise. But her hostility was melting. A grudging interest took its place. "Are your shoes made of used tires, from cars, or what?" she asked Mizz Z.

"Not from cars," Mizz Z corrected her. "But from a wrecked army jeep. You see, we are both concerned about recycling."

"So where'd you buy shoes like that?" demanded Frankie, with something like envy in her voice. "Are they on eBay?"

"What about this mudball?" demanded Jin, jigging about impatiently. "You said we shouldn't waste time. You said it was dangerous."

"Ah, yes," said Mizz Z, turning her amber eye toward him, as if she'd forgotten what they were here for.

"Mudball?" echoed Frankie. She, too, switched her gaze to Jin. "Didn't you say something about a mudball before? Look, what's going on?"

So Jin told her. He gabbled out the story, or as much as Mizz Z had told him. Frankie didn't react much. She hated showing surprise because that wasn't cool. But even her eyes widened a little.

She turned to Mizz Z. "Is this true?" she demanded. "It sounds crazy."

"Unfortunately, it is true," confirmed Mizz Z. "But don't worry. We at RAAAA are well trained to deal with such things. And Zilombo and I have met before. In fact, you might say, this is not just a routine job for me. This is personal."

And as she said this, Mizz Z's hand stole up again to stroke that black eye patch.

"Zilombo?" said Jin, wrinkling his nose in confusion. "Who's that?"

"Ahhh, did I not say?" said Mizz Z.

"No, you didn't," said Jin.

"Can someone explain about this Zilombo dude?" demanded Frankie, putting down her can of red spray paint. "'Cos I haven't got a clue either."

Mizz Z hesitated. She looked at the gray, swirling Oozeburn, getting higher as the tide rose. Then she said mysteriously, "Well, she must have hatched already. So a few seconds will not make any difference."

Mizz Z sank down gracefully on her heels. She beckoned Jin and Frankie to sit beside her among the weeds and brambles.

"When I was a little girl," said Mizz Z, "we lived on the edge of a great lake in Malawi. And my mum would tell me a story about Zilombo. The story came from long, long ago, from the far-off days of myths and magic. Anyway, back then, so the story said, a hideous creature lived in our lake. People called her Zilombo, which means *beasts* because, in truth, she was a mixture of many. Some things about her seemed human. But then she had teeth like a crocodile, skin like a hippo, a leap like a frog, and swivel eyes like a chameleon. And she could do what a lungfish does.

In times of drought, she would shrink herself down in size, bury herself in the riverbed, wrap a ball of mud around her and wait . . ."

"Wait for the water to come back!" Jin said, in an appalled whisper.

"Exactly right." Mizz Z nodded. "And then Zilombo would hatch out of her mudball, even stronger and bigger and more powerful than before. But Zilombo had another croc habit. Did you know that crocodiles keep a food store in their dens?"

Jin shook his head, trying to ignore the sick, twisting feeling that was coiling like a snake deep inside his guts.

"I did," Frankie surprised him by saying. "I read that somewhere."

"Well, Zilombo did that too," Mizz Z continued. "Usually she ate *chambo*."

"Ate *what*?" said Frankie.

"*Chambo*," explained Mizz Z. "That is our Chewa word for the fish that live in our lake. Anyhow, Zilombo speared them on her long toe- and finger-nails. But she was very greedy. She kept a food store in case her *chambo* supply ran out. But Zilombo was more fussy than crocs. She liked to keep her food fresh and alive . . ."

"What kind of food?" asked Frankie.

Mizz Z hesitated. "Gazelles," she said, "who came down to drink at the lake edge. Or baby wildebeest."

"Yeah, well, there's loads of those round here, isn't there?" said Frankie, rolling her eyes.

Mizz Z ignored Frankie's sarcastic comment. Her own voice stayed deadly serious. "Well, according to the story, babies of any kind would do," she continued.

Jin felt the blood drain from his face: "You saying what I think you're saying? That she even scoffed *children*!"

"Sometimes," nodded Mizz Z. "So the old stories said."

"Only witches in fairy tales scoff children!" Frankie laughed.

"Zilombo is no witch," said Mizz Z firmly. "And she is no fairy tale, either. Besides, it is not at all surprising. Crocodiles sometimes snatched children from the riverbank. So did lions and hyenas. And Zilombo is more beast than human."

Frankie snorted a scornful "Huh!" as if Mizz Z was talking rubbish. But Jin noticed that she was twisting the frills on her frock tightly round her arms, like black bandages. She didn't even seem to know she was doing it.

Mizz Z fixed Frankie with her single amber eye. "Yes, I thought it was rubbish too," she told her. "I thought it was just another old story to frighten children. There were many like that in my village. But then I was out playing with my little brother. He was three years old, hardly more than a baby. He was digging in a riverbed that had been dry since anyone could remember. Anyway, I wasn't watching him like I should. He dug up a ball of mud. He started to play football with it, kicking it about. He kicked it toward the lake. I heard his necklace jangling as he ran after it. I had made that necklace for him, out of Fanta bottle tops . . ."

"Oh no!" Jin interrupted her, his eyes wide with horror. He could see where this story was leading.

"Zilombo didn't . . ." he spluttered, hardly able to get out the words. "She didn't scoff your baby brother?"

"Baby brother?" Frankie suddenly echoed, gazing round. "Has anyone seen Smiler?"

Jin shot to his feet, fighting off the brambles that tried to ensnare him. "Smiler!" he shouted, his heart thudding wildly. "What's he doing here? I thought he was at home!"

Now Frankie was really rattled. Her words came out all in a rush. "I rang Mum, you heard me, about that letter Grandma and Grandad Tang got, and she came rushing over in the car and drove them off somewhere—to Citizens Advice, I think—and anyway she left Smiler for me to look after and I was spray painting and I forgot all about him!"

Jin stared at her, aghast. "You forgot about Smiler? I can't believe you'd do that!"

But to his surprise Mizz Z sprang to Frankie's defense. "This is no time for blame," she said briskly. "This is a time for action. Now tell me, Frankie. Where is the last place you saw your little brother?"

CHAPTER

SIX

Goo!" gurgled Smiler, spreading his pudgy fingers like a starfish, to show off his drool cat's cradle.

Zilombo turned one of her cold, green eyes briefly in his direction. She was squatting with her back to him, sucking the juices from a flapping fish skewered on a spearlike fingernail. But those swivel eyes could see even behind her.

Smiler didn't know what was going on. One second he'd been crawling along the Oozeburn's banks, sniffing at interesting smells, poking his finger into interesting holes. The next second he'd been snatched away. Smiler was used to people picking him up, cooing in his face. Everyone wanted to cuddle such a smiley baby. But this person was different. She had slimy skin, for a start, and a strong fishy stink. He'd smiled at her, like he did to everyone. But instead of smiling back, her cold fishy eyes had glittered and she'd pulled back her lips in a snarl to show gleaming, pointy fangs.

Smiler started to whimper, screwing his fists around in his eyes. He wished he had Bobo, his tatty old toy monkey, to comfort him. It was dark and cold inside the old sewage pipe, the place Zilombo had chosen for her den. The only light came through the grid. Zilombo had kicked it out with one big foot to get inside. Then she'd rammed it wonkily back in the pipe entrance so she had a front door.

Zilombo chucked a dead rat over her shoulder at Smiler. Was it to shut him up? Or so he could eat it and stay alive until she wanted to eat *him*? Who knew what was in Zilombo's mind? She was a very, very ancient creature. She'd been on Earth for millions of years. Either feasting in lakes and streams or hibernating inside her ball of dried mud. Sometimes, she'd had to wait centuries for water to release her.

But now that she was free again, she was going to stuff her belly.

Tiny red crabs scuttled endlessly through her mane and in and out of the folds of her baggy, gray skin. She grabbed one, popped it into her mouth, and crunched it.

Zilombo had many itchy places. She put her arm over her back and scratched one. It sounded like nails scraping down sandpaper. She shook her matted hair. Crabs flew out and river weed and shining fish scales.

"Oooo," said Smiler. He stopped whimpering and crawled over to have a look at the half-gnawed rat, jabbing it with his finger.

When the tide had come in, Zilombo had hatched completely, swelling to her full size. She was seven feet tall, a giantess. She'd come bursting up from the mud like a guided missile. Her rumbling belly sounded like an underground train. She'd crouched thigh-deep in water, searching for fish. Her toes were handy for little jobs, like strangling seagulls. But her webbed hands were far deadlier weapons. They had long, sharp talons, which were curled into leopard claws.

There! Her eyes had taken on a sharkish glint. She'd pounced. Stabbed ferociously: one, two, three times. Then her hands had come up, dripping from the water, with six silvery, gasping fish shish kebabbed on her fingernails.

Zilombo had licked her chops greedily. Then she'd started chomping.

It was a good thing for Smiler that Zilombo had taken the edge off her hunger before she snatched him: that she was saving him for when her fish supply ran out.

Up on the towpath, Jin and Frankie were panicking. "We've got to find Smiler," wailed Frankie, "before Mum comes back! She'll kill me! I was supposed to be looking after him!"

Only Mizz Z stayed cool. She looked down from the towpath, searching for places that Zilombo might choose as a den. Opposite them, set in the brick wall, was a huge iron grid, about a meter above the waterline.

"What is that?" she asked Jin, pointing across to the grid.

"It's the cover over an old sewage pipe," Jin told her. "See that ladder just near it? That goes right down the wall. I climbed down that ladder once and looked through the grid. There's this dark tunnel behind it—that's the pipe. It's massive; a kid could stand up in there."

"A dark tunnel?" said Mizz Z. "That would suit Zilombo perfectly."

"That's how you get to the other side," said Jin, pointing out a rusty iron footbridge that crossed the Oozeburn, almost hidden by overhanging willow trees.

Jin expected Mizz Z to stride across the bridge, climb down the ladder and check out the pipe for herself. But she didn't. She seemed to be hesitating.

Jin stared at her face, surprised. He wasn't brilliant at some things: football or riding a bike, for instance. But he was expert at other things. Like being wary and watchful, noting the tiniest change in people's faces. Because when your coordination's not great and you can't fight or run away, being super alert to people's moods is your best protection. And Jin had spied a nerve twitching in Mizz Z's cheek, right under her black eye patch.

Could it be a flicker of fear?

I hope not, he thought. Because if the formidable Mizz Z was afraid, then this Zilombo must be a truly fearsome creature, something from your worst nightmares.

But then the flicker vanished, as fast as it had come. And soon Jin wasn't even sure he'd seen it.

Mizz Z's voice was clear and loud. It rang like a gong between the derelict buildings. "Hey!" she shouted. "Hey! Come out, if you are in there!"

For a few seconds there was silence. Nothing moved except the swirling water. Then suddenly the grid exploded from the channel wall. Jin nearly leaped out his skin. Zilombo had booted it out with one big flat foot—a foot that could have been human, except for the webbed toes and savage yellow talons.

Then a leg followed the foot. A leg Jin recognized well, like a giant chicken's with gray scaly skin. Its ankle bracelet, made of Fanta bottle tops, rattled furiously.

And Jin thought, with a shudder: *Did that bracelet once belong to Mizz Z's baby brother?*

Frankie gasped. "What on earth is *that*?"

"Meet Zilombo," came Mizz Z's cool reply. "She used to be in a mudball on top of Madalitso's wardrobe."

A head poked out of the great, gaping hole. It had the low, jutting forehead of an ape. The nose was pulled forward into a muzzle, like a dog. Fish guts dribbled from lips as thin as a snake's. Eyes swiveled toward them.

Zilombo raised her head and sniffed the air. Like a shark, she had poor eyesight. But her sense of smell was as keen as a wolf. And she smelled fresh meat.

She grunted eagerly. Then stuck out her head a bit more to get a better sniff. Frankie saw her gray hippo skin and neck, baggy as a walrus. Her rusty orange hair, slimed with river weed, stuck up in a crest on her head, Mohawk style, then bristled down her back like a lion's mane.

She was a hideous mutant, a mixture of many beasts. But when that dreadful head turned in his direction, stared at him, Jin's already pounding heart almost stopped. He was ace at reading faces. And he saw something human in Zilombo, in those shifty green eyes under that jutting brow.

But that thought immediately vanished from his mind. Because Zilombo turned her huge bulk back into the pipe. She appeared again almost instantly, with something dangling from a hooked claw on her webbed hand.

"Smiler!" shrieked Frankie, clamping a hand to her mouth to stop herself shrieking again.

Those horny yellow nails held Smiler by the straps of his overalls, swung him out over the water. His legs and arms scrabbled frantically like a cockroach, as if he was trying to crawl away.

Zilombo seemed to find his desperate escape attempts funny. A weird sound came up from her thick baggy neck. It sounded like the squawk of a heron.

"Zilombo is laughing," Mizz Z explained.

Zilombo howled again as Smiler's legs pedaled

in midair. Her saggy belly shook with amusement. Shrimps flew out of the folds in her skin.

"Let my brother go!" shrieked Frankie. "You freak!"

"I'm going to get him!" yelled Jin, dashing toward the iron bridge.

"No!" ordered Mizz Z urgently. "Wait!"

Zilombo started her war dance. She stomped her feet and made her ankle bracelet rattle menacingly.

Horrified, Jin saw Smiler bounce up and down, as if he was on elastic. But Zilombo didn't drop him in the water. That would be a waste. Instead, she put him down, behind her, inside the pipe. Then she really went berserk. Her whole body appeared, crouched in the pipe's entrance. Her great flat feet stamped out a beat as the bottle tops shook: *clang, rattle, clang, rattle.* She pounded her chest with her cupped hands like King Kong in a rage. It made a sound like a big bass drum: *boom, boom!* Then she started pelting things at them across the Oozeburn, anything she could lay her hands on: dead rats, fish bones, bricks she clawed out of the wall.

As missiles came hurtling down, Mizz Z showed

her amazing strength. She hauled up a rusty sheet of corrugated iron that had been dumped beside the towpath. She just ripped it straight out of the earth. Wood lice, lizards, and grass snakes scattered in all directions.

"Take cover!" she cried, holding the sheet up like a shield.

They huddled beneath it as bricks thudded around them. Jin flinched as one clanged off the metal. And all the time Zilombo was shrieking and howling in pure animal fury.

Then suddenly she paused in her attack.

Her short-sighted eyes peered up at the towpath. She grunted in satisfaction. She couldn't see the intruders anymore. They seemed to have run away. Her little explosion of rage, hardly more than a hissy fit, had made her peckish and she fancied a snack. But she'd thrown all her *chambo* and dead rats across the Ooozeburn. Never mind. This was where a food store came in handy. She snaked out an arm behind her to grab Smiler. Her long nails stabbed about. But they didn't spear anything.

Zilombo gazed at her empty talons.

She twisted her whole body round and croaked angrily into the darkness. No answer. Her brow creased up in confusion. Zilombo was a merciless predator. Even humans were her prey. But she was a very slow thinker.

At last she realized what must have happened. She threw back her great beast's head and let out a howl of outrage.

Her food store had legged it. Another furious howl echoed along the Oozeburn. Then there was silence.

After a few minutes, Mizz Z laid down the metal sheet. She'd been holding it high above them and even her arms were trembling with the weight.

"Is it safe?" stammered Jin as they crouched among the brambles, his ears still ringing from the brick battering and Zilombo's savage shrieks.

"No," said Mizz Z. "When Zilombo escapes, it is never safe."

"But what about Smiler?" demanded Frankie. She was close to tears. Jin had never seen his big sister break down like this. He didn't blame her; he was almost hysterical himself.

"If that monster eats Smiler . . ." he raved. He clenched his fists. "I'll, I'll—" But what could he do? He let his fists dangle helplessly. His face twisted up in distress and horror.

"*Shhh!*" said Mizz Z. "I am thinking."

"But—!" interrupted Jin.

"*Shhh!*" said Mizz Z again. "This is what we inspectors are trained for."

So they waited. It seemed like forever, although it was only a few seconds. Jin couldn't keep still. His legs twitched, as if they had a life of their own. Frankie tugged a black frill around her wrist so tightly it cut into her skin. But she didn't even notice the pain.

Finally Mizz Z announced, "OK. To rescue your brother, I must sneak into Zilombo's den the back way. Now where does that old sewer pipe lead to? Are there any other ways down there?"

Jin shook his head hopelessly. He hadn't a clue. But Frankie did. "I know another way down!" she said. "But we have to cross the Oozeburn first."

"Not by that iron bridge," said Mizz Z. "It is too close to Zilombo's den."

"Don't worry," shouted Frankie, already racing along the bank. "There's a wooden bridge round the corner. Come on!"

"Excellent," said Mizz Z as she and Jin ran to catch up.

CHAPTER
SEVEN

While Zilombo was working herself up into a steaming frenzy, stomping, screaming, pelting rocks like a giant angry gorilla, Smiler had sat behind her wailing, his fingers plugged in his ears.

But then he'd seen something down the pipe, in the black distance. It glowed green. It sparkled like a jewel.

"Oooo!" Smiler had marveled, his blue eyes round with wonder. Immediately he'd forgotten his distress. With a determined baby crawl, he'd made his way toward it, disappearing into the dark.

As Zilombo's shrieks and howls, the thumping

drumbeat of her feet, had faded behind him, Smiler forgot about her. His entire baby brain was concentrated on one thing. Getting his chubby mitts on that shiny treasure.

And here it was.

Smiler didn't know, but it was called a *slime mold*, a kind of fungus that glows in the dark. It flowed down the wall like green ice cream. It threw its eerie green light on Smiler's face. He grinned at it, tried to grab it. But it was high above him. Never mind. There were more slime molds ahead of him, growing inside the pipe like a sinister midnight garden. One dripped neon orange. One, far ahead, was white and glimmered in the dark like ice crystals.

Gurgling with pleasure, Smiler headed for it. He had a very fast crawl, especially when it was to grab something he wanted. With his spiky hair, he looked like a running hedgehog as he scuttled along in the gloom, lit only by the slime mold's creepy glow.

He didn't see, scattered between the slime molds, several red Chinese dragons, spray painted on the walls, each one with spiky flames in the shape of an F coming out of its mouth.

He didn't notice either, as he raced along, that one of his cute blue denim baby boots fell off and got left behind. A passing rat sniffed at it, its eyes burning red in the gloom. Then it scurried off, squeaking, on some mission of its own.

On the other side of the Oozeburn was a modern and very swish hotel. It soared above the crumbling factories, its windows blazing like fire in the late afternoon sun. Chauffeured limos purred up to its doors, letting out people with posh matching luggage.

"This way!" yelled Frankie as she pushed through its glass revolving doors, followed by Mizz Z. "This is a shortcut to where we want to be!"

Frankie's biker boots pounded across the lobby. Behind her, Mizz Z's army jeep flip-flops whack-whacked on the slippery, polished floor.

Behind *them*, Jin was trapped in the revolving door, helplessly spinning round and round, as if he was in a washing machine. He saw a gap, dived for it and ended up skidding across the lobby floor like an ice dancer, before collapsing in a heap by the lifts.

Jin never let little accidents like that put him off. Dizzily he lurched after Frankie and Mizz Z. "Hey, you two, wait for me!" he yelled, trying to stop himself going round in circles.

The smart lady behind the desk gaped at the bizarre trio: the wild-looking girl in a black party dress, the spectacular Mizz Z, the boy staggering behind them. She picked up the hotel phone and said, "Get me Security!"

But by then Frankie had led Jin and Mizz Z away from the front lobby, through a maze of narrow, airless corridors meant for cleaning staff. She pushed at a fire door and they burst out into the sunshine. They were in scrubby, rubble-strewn wasteland at the back of the hotel, a piece of land that had been forgotten. Just the kind of place Frankie felt at home in.

"Over here!" she yelled.

When Jin reached them, scrambling over piles of old bricks, Mizz Z and Frankie were staring at what looked like a big manhole cover with a metal wheel set in it.

"That wheel is to open and close it," said Frankie. "There's an iron ladder underneath that leads down to the old sewer pipe."

Mizz Z didn't ask how she knew. It was obvious Frankie had been here before. Her tag, the red Chinese dragon, was spray painted everywhere.

Mizz Z merely said, "Then I shall go down there and get your brother back."

She said it in a casual, almost offhand way, as if it was just part of her day's work as the chief inspector. Only Jin, with his brilliant face-reading skills, saw that nerve flicker again under her black eye patch. And knew she was afraid. He felt a sudden tug of sympathy. It made Mizz Z seem more like an ordinary person. Not some kind of superwoman.

"Maybe we should go for help?" he suggested.

Mizz Z glanced at him sideways, as if she'd suddenly remembered that this kid was sharper than he looked.

"That is totally out of the question," she said,

tossing her head haughtily. It seemed her superb self-confidence had returned. "Every so often we at RAAAA have little problems like this. It is no big deal. It is part of my job." She unslung her backpack. "This will just get in my way," she said.

Jin threw himself on the wheel that opened the manhole cover. With all his strength he tried to wrench it round. But it wouldn't budge. Beads of sweat broke out on his forehead.

"Wrong way," said Mizz Z, moving him gently to one side. Her powerful arms hauled the wheel to the left. With a grating sound it turned. Mizz Z lifted the lid, threw it aside. All of them peered down the deep hole beneath. As Frankie had said, an iron ladder disappeared down into darkness.

Jin's mind was going manic. It kept showing him nightmare pictures of what might be happening to Smiler. *Don't go there, don't go there,* he told himself, blocking out those awful images.

Then he heard Frankie telling Mizz Z, "You won't fit in the pipe. It's narrow down there. It only gets wide near the Oozeburn end." In the panic about

Smiler she'd forgotten about details like that.

"How do you know this?" demanded Mizz Z, who was just about to go down the ladder.

"Because I've crawled through the pipe," Frankie blurted out. "From here to the grid and back again. I forgot about how narrow it was this end. You definitely wouldn't fit."

"I would, though!" said Jin. He was already hurling himself toward the hole. Mum always warned him: "Think of the risks!" But this was no time for thinking. Not when Zilombo had captured Smiler.

He started clambering down the ladder.

"No, Jin!" shrieked Frankie. "I'll go! You'll only fall! Stop him!" she appealed to Mizz Z. "He's dyspraxic!"

"*Pah!*" said Mizz Z, with another scornful toss of her head. "What is that word? I do not even know what it means." But she shouted stern instructions to Jin as he made his way down. "Only go to the bottom," she called. "Look along the pipe and report back. Make sure you obey me!"

"OK!" came Jin's muffled voice.

"Watch out for that Zilombo!" bawled Frankie.

Mizz Z turned to reassure Frankie. "There is no risk. If the pipe is narrow, then Zilombo can't get through to this end. Do you think I would have let him go otherwise? But neither can I get through to her. It is rather annoying. I shall have to change my plans . . ."

"Rather annoying!" Frankie was shrieking, her face twisted in distress. "Is that all you can say? That monster's got my baby brother! And it's all my fault! Do you know what that feels like?"

Mizz Z didn't shout back. Instead, she did a very peculiar thing. Frankie wasn't a huggable girl. If her family had tried, she'd have scowled, "Gerroff! Leave me alone!" and bristled like a porcupine. But Mizz Z didn't hesitate. She folded Frankie in her arms and stroked her hair to comfort her.

"As it happens," said Mizz Z gently as Frankie collapsed in tears, "we have something in common. Because I know *exactly* what that feels like." Then suddenly Mizz Z let Frankie go. Her voice was full of steely determination. "But we do not give up hope," she told Frankie. "That is not allowed! We never give up hope."

As Jin went farther down into the dark, Frankie's anguished shouts faded. The hole where the iron ladder went down was lined with bricks. Jin's fingers brushed them as he was groping for handholds. They were wet and slimy with seeping water. Roots, like white worms, poked through from the trees and plants growing on the wasteland above.

Whoops, Jin thought, hanging on for dear life. He'd just carefully lowered his foot, scrabbling for the next slippery rung, and there wasn't one. Had he reached the bottom of the hole? He lowered his foot farther and, to his huge relief, found solid ground.

He stepped off the ladder. It was like being at the bottom of a well. Far above him he could see a pale disk of daylight. *Did I climb all the way down from there?* he thought wonderingly as he gazed back up the ladder. *Without falling off, or hardly putting a foot wrong?* That was a massive achievement. But he was too worried about Smiler to feel pleased with himself.

Mizz Z's voice floated down: "Are you OK?"

"Yeah, fine!" Jin yelled back, surprised at how little his voice shook.

And that must be the pipe—that great round hole in the brick wall. He crouched down, peered in. Frankie was right, the pipe was much narrower here than at the Oozeburn end. But it wasn't a pitch-black tunnel, like he'd expected. There were strange things glowing dimly at the far end, different colors, like fuzzy Christmas lights.

His mind was just puzzling—*What are they?*— when he saw something moving.

His whole body suddenly went icy cold. "Zilombo," he whispered through chattering teeth.

Just as he remembered she wouldn't fit through the pipe, he saw Smiler, lit up in the ghostly white glow of a slime mold. He was padding along on all fours, like a little wolf cub out exploring, sniffing at this, licking that.

"Smiler!" yelled Jin, joy crashing through him like a huge, foamy wave. "Smiler, it's me—Jin!"

Smiler turned his face toward Jin. His eyes crinkled into a grin. He gave his usual cheery greeting, "Goo!" and wagged his hand about.

As Mizz Z and Frankie leaned to look down the hole, a deliriously happy voice floated up to them. "Smiler's here! He's OK! I've found him!"

Meanwhile, Zilombo was in hot pursuit of her food store, first crawling, then slithering behind Smiler through the pipe. He was some way ahead. But she wasn't too worried. There was no way he could escape.

She kept her snout down, sniffing. Once she lapped like a dog at a puddle of stinking, scummy water. Her long tongue was gray and furry.

Then she became aware that the pipe was shrinking. She was already touching its metal walls. But the slime molds greased her orange mane and her thick, wrinkly hippo hide. She was able to slide a few meters farther.

Then her yellow talons felt something. She snatched it up. It was a little baby boot, pale blue denim with red laces. She sniffed it all over, especially inside, where Smiler's personal smell was strongest.

She snarled softly, drawing her lips back and

showing white, snaggled fangs. She had two rows of teeth, like a crocodile. And if one got wobbly, from too much bone crunching, she'd just yank it out. And, like a croc, another tooth quickly grew in its place.

She tore Smiler's boot to shreds in her teeth, shaking it like a Rottweiler, then spat it out.

Now that she'd smelled her prey, her ferocity doubled. Where food was concerned Zilombo never, ever, gave up. She tried to force herself farther, ram herself through the pipe.

With a shriek of rage she knew she wouldn't fit. The chase was over. She couldn't go any farther.

Then something amazing happened. Even Zilombo's slow brain found it surprising. She seemed to be getting skinnier, sort of folding up inside. It was a very peculiar feeling.

"Ugh?" she grunted, puzzled.

Each time she hatched, Zilombo became more deadly. She evolved new predator's skills, like her wolf smell, her croc teeth. And now she'd discovered her latest talent. She could collapse her skeleton like a rat. Rats can wriggle through the tiniest holes. As long as they can fit their skull through, they can squash their other bones, so the rest of their body will follow.

She gave another grunt, this time of triumph.

Again, she thrust her great shaggy beast head forward. And, to her delight, the rest of her came too, like toothpaste squeezed through a tube.

Frightful squawks burst from her new slim-line body. Zilombo was laughing. She thought it was an excellent joke. Her food store thought it had escaped. But soon, very soon, she would catch up with it.

CHAPTER
EIGHT

"Come on, Smiler," coaxed Jin. "Come here."

Jin was crouched at the bottom of the iron ladder, peering along the pipe to where Smiler was playing with the slime molds.

Smiler was a very stubborn baby. He wouldn't come until he was ready. But Jin couldn't feel panicky. All he felt was a warm, pink glow of pleasure inside him because he'd found Smiler, safe and unharmed. He just couldn't stop grinning about it.

"It is time to bring that baby up," Mizz Z called down from the surface.

"We're coming," Jin called back. "But it's OK.

Frankie's right—the pipe's narrow at this end. There's no way Zilombo can get through. Not a chance."

Mizz Z replied, "That is good news." It seemed, for the moment at least, the panic was over—they were safe.

So why did Mizz Z suddenly hear a grim, warning voice at the back of her mind: *Never, ever, underestimate Zilombo.*

"I think you should bring him up now," called Mizz Z, a little more urgently.

From a few meters along the pipe, Smiler said "Goo!" and waved one hand about again. This time *Goo* meant: "Come and see what I've found!" Smiler was a very friendly and sociable baby. He liked to share his toys with everyone.

Jin sighed. He knew he'd have to go and fetch his baby brother. On hands and knees he crawled into the pipe. Smiler was sitting down now, his face lit by a ghoulish green glow. He was enchanted by the best slime mold he'd found so far. It dripped down the pipe wall like luminous green snot. And, what was best of all, he could reach it.

Smiler dabbed his finger in it, raised the finger to his mouth.

"No!" said Jin, reaching him just in time to grab his chubby fist. "*Yuck!* Don't eat that! Nasty!"

Jin's voice boomed in the metal pipe. When it had finished echoing—"*Nasty-nasty-nasty*"—there was an eerie silence.

Suddenly Jin felt the skin crawl on the back of his neck. He shivered. Then grinned at his own fear. What did he feel so jittery about? There was no danger. Zilombo couldn't get through. And the mighty Mizz Z was close by, just at the top of the ladder.

Smiler was chuckling too. He sped off, back down the pipe, fast as a newly hatched baby turtle scuttling down to the sea.

"Don't mess me about, Smiler!" yelled Jin. "I'm not playing Chasey!"

Then Jin heard a familiar sound. At first he couldn't believe it. He thought his ears were playing tricks. His reason told him, "No, it can't be!"

Then it came again, that spine-chilling shake of Fanta bottle tops.

Jin felt sick. His stomach was trampolining. Trembling, he stared farther down the pipe, into the blackness, beyond Smiler's crawling figure.

He couldn't see anything. But he was sure there was something there. Something awful was approaching. He could feel it in the air.

"Smiler!" he hissed. "Come back!"

Smiler stopped. He sat on his bottom and grinned. Any second, he would take off again.

"Smiler!" begged Jin desperately.

Then he saw her eyes, twin fiery green beams like the headlamps of an underground train, speeding toward them along the pipe.

For a few seconds, Jin froze completely. His brain tried to deny what was happening.

Then, "Zilombo!" he roared. But Smiler was off again, in the wrong direction. Jin hurled himself toward the crawling baby, grabbed a stripy sock. To his horror, the sock peeled off in his hand. "Smiler! Stay here!" He lunged for Smiler's foot, missed. But found the strap of his overalls.

And all the time Smiler was gurgling in happy

excitement, as if this was a terrific game.

Jin started dragging Smiler back along the pipe. Smiler's bottom bumped on the metal but his thick, padded diaper stopped him from getting hurt. Still, Smiler yelled in protest. He didn't want to leave. He liked it down here, in his twinkly slime-mold fairyland.

On the surface, Mizz Z and Frankie heard Jin's warning shout.

They stared at each other, aghast. "Did he say Zilombo?" asked Frankie, her voice shaky with shock and disbelief.

Mizz Z sprang into action first. She was already stepping onto the first rung of the iron ladder before Frankie reacted.

"I'm coming too," declared Frankie.

"No!" commanded Mizz Z as she started climbing down. "You stay here. Keep an eye on my laptop. It contains many of RAAAA's secret files."

Frankie hated taking orders. But she stayed where she was, crouched at the top, watching Mizz Z's brightly colored head wrap bobbing down into the gloom.

With Smiler in his grasp, Jin crawled out of the pipe. He scrambled to his feet, glanced up the iron ladder, saw Mizz Z's flip-flops descending.

"Zi-Zi-lombo!" shuddered Jin though chattering teeth. "She got through!"

He could smell decaying crabs now and hear that angry rattle, horribly close.

"I'll take the baby!" said Mizz Z. She scooped a wailing Smiler up from the ground, then pushed Jin onto the ladder. "Climb! Quickly!"

Jin climbed, his breath coming out in great gasping sobs, groping wildly for handholds and footholds, desperate not to hold up Mizz Z, climbing behind him.

It had seemed like a long way down. But it was even longer going up. He slipped, clung frantically to the ladder. His legs seemed to have lost all strength. They felt as limp as cooked noodles, and his palms were so slippery with sweat he couldn't hold on.

I'm going to fall! he thought in a panic. But, to his amazement, inside his head there was part of him still in control. "You will not fall!" he told himself in a voice that sounded awfully like Mizz Z at her strictest. "Carry on! You will make it!"

Jin's legs were wobbly, his blood roaring in his ears. But he carried on climbing. And he did make it.

A few rungs from the top, arms reached down to help him. Frankie hauled him out. Then she grabbed Smiler as Mizz Z thrust him out of the hole, and put him down on a heap of rubble.

"Don't you dare move!" Frankie warned her baby brother.

Smiler stopped howling and started playing with the bricks.

Mizz Z, still on the ladder, looked down. Zilombo's muzzle appeared, poking out of the pipe below, sniffing the ground. Then Mizz Z saw her shaggy lion's mane. Zilombo raised her head. Her brutal face, part human but mostly beast, gazed upward. Her tiny shark eyes gleamed with rage.

Did Zilombo recognize Mizz Z as the little girl who, all those years ago, had tried to steal her prey once before? Mizz Z didn't wait to find out. She grabbed the metal lid, slammed it back in place.

"Help me!" she panted.

The three of them fought to turn the rusty wheel that locked the lid. Finally it grated into place. Not a second too soon. For Zilombo had squeezed herself out of the pipe and come swarming up the ladder.

They heard her long talons raking against the lid, trying to claw her way through to get at them. Now she was booting the lid with one great flat foot—*boom, boom, boom!*—like a battering ram.

The ground shook like a mini earthquake. The metal lid dented. Would it survive Zilombo's savage kicking? Frankie chewed her black glossy nails.

"How did she get through? How did she get through?" Jin kept asking in a dazed, trembling voice.

Then the lid lifted slightly, right at the edge. Two long yellow talons slid through, scrabbling around. Bloodthirsty howls came through the gap.

"Run!" cried Jin. Frankie snatched Smiler up.

"Wait!" said Mizz Z. She wasn't running away. To their amazement, she was walking *toward* the lid. Crouching by it, careful to avoid those stabbing claws, she put her face as close as she could to the gap. And began a crooning song, jingling her bronze bangles, tapping her feet softly to its dreamy, hypnotic beat.

"What are you *doing*?" begged Frankie.

"*Shhh!*" whispered Mizz Z.

She carried on singing. Slowly the ferocious kicking ceased. Gradually the howls faded. At last there was silence under the lid, as if Zilombo was listening.

Mizz Z crooned on. Her low, drowsy voice and the sleepy, repetitive rhythm had Jin's eyelids drooping.

He snapped back awake when another sound came from beneath the lid. A sort of deep rumbling, rising and falling, like underground thunder.

Mizz Z stopped singing. She listened for a long time. Finally satisfied, she rose to her feet.

"Zilombo is snoring," she announced. "She has climbed back down to the bottom of the hole, where she is taking a nap."

"Taking a nap?" said Jin, in disbelief. "But ten seconds ago, she sounded like she wanted to rip us to shreds!"

"I sang her a very ancient lullaby," announced

Mizz Z briskly. "And it made her drowsy. Finally she fell asleep. We are safe, for the moment."

"How'd you know it would work?" asked Jin, amazed.

"I have my own reasons," said Mizz Z mysteriously. "Anyway, we should go, in case she wakes up." But first, Mizz Z heaved a big slab of concrete from the pile of rubble and lowered it quietly over the tiny gap Zilombo had made.

"Think she'll try to get out through the lid when she wakes up?" asked Jin.

Mizz Z shook her head. "I'm just taking precautions. I think she'll go back down the pipe again, guard her den from the Oozeburn end. After all, that's where the fish are."

Then Frankie spoke up: "I've got to take Smiler to Grandma Tang's. I'm supposed to be there, looking after him. What if Mum comes back to find us gone?"

"But that's where Zilombo's den entrance is!" protested Jin. "Right opposite their back door."

"There's another door, round the front of the factory," Frankie explained to Mizz Z. "But I only have a key to the back door. So we have to go past Zilombo's den."

"That is no problem," shrugged Mizz Z. "While Zilombo is napping here, we can go past her den in perfect safety. But this flat you speak of, is it on the ground floor?"

Frankie shook her head. "It's on the fifth floor. Right at the top of the building."

"Good," nodded Mizz Z. "We should be safe up there. Zilombo is very territorial. She hardly ever strays far from her den."

At least, the Zilombo Mizz Z had known as a girl didn't. But would this newly hatched Zilombo be different? While in the mudball she'd evolved some formidable skills. Now she could squeeze through very narrow spaces to catch her prey. What other nasty surprises did she have in store? Mizz Z tried to put these disturbing thoughts to the back of her mind.

"Anyway, we shall go to this flat," decided Mizz Z. "And I shall make a plan to recapture Zilombo." She slung on her backpack and strode off, her head held high.

"Go, Mizz Z!" whispered Jin. With his sharp eyes, he'd seen that nerve flutter again, just below her eye patch. Only he knew she was secretly afraid. But she didn't show it. She looked like she could take on the world!

"Come on," said Frankie, grabbing Smiler, who was collecting slugs off the bricks and cramming them in the pocket of his overalls.

Jin still hadn't gotten an answer to his question. "But how did she get through that pipe?" he asked as he panted after Mizz Z.

"I don't know," was Mizz Z's frank reply. "Zilombo is indeed a marvelous creature."

"Marvelous?" protested Frankie. "She's a monster!"

They took the shortcut back through the hotel.

"Security!" shrieked the smart receptionist into the phone. "They're back. Only now they've got a baby with them!"

Smiler was a heavy baby. In the lobby, Frankie plonked him down to give her aching arms a rest. Smiler crawled after her, shedding slugs from the pockets of his overalls. Some were squashed accidentally by Jin. Others made a bid for freedom, leaving sticky silver slime trails all over the polished floor.

"Goo!" said Smiler as he crawled past the smart receptionist. His eyes crinkled in a friendly fashion. He held up his favorite to show her—a big orange tiger slug with yellow stripes.

The smart receptionist shuddered in disgust. A security guy dressed in a blue uniform with gold braid appeared out of the lift.

"Wait!" he barked self-importantly. "You there! I want a word with you."

Mizz Z stopped, turned her head. She didn't need to say a thing. One fierce golden flash from her eye was enough. It seemed to say, "Are you talking to me?" The security guy took the hint. He melted back into the lift. Mizz Z strode on, haughty as a queen.

Jin was prepared this time for those revolving doors. He only went round in them twice before he spilled out on the pavement. But Smiler raced toward them, grinning with delight. He wanted to go round in them too.

"No, you don't," said Frankie, scooping him up as he howled in protest.

They crossed again by the wooden bridge and hurried along the towpath. But as they neared Zilombo's den, Mizz Z held up a warning hand.

"Stay here, you children," she whispered. She crept stealthily ahead of them. She stared across at the opposite bank. But there was no Zilombo guarding the den entrance. Was she still slumbering, like a giant snoring baby, at the far end of the pipe?

"Is she there?" Frankie called out softly.

"I can't see her," answered Mizz Z. But then, to Jin's alarm, she began sneaking across the iron bridge.

"What are you *doing*?" he hissed. "Come back."

"I must check that there is no danger," came Mizz Z's voice from the other side of the Oozeburn.

But she didn't just check from the bank. She climbed halfway down the long ladder attached to the brick wall. The scummy water of the Oozeburn swirled just below her.

"Be careful," Jin begged.

Mizz Z leaned across, looking right into the den.

"What can you see?" asked Frankie.

Mizz Z called back, her voice much louder now. "I see some stinking fish guts. And a well-chewed rat. But it is OK. Zilombo is not at home."

Mizz Z came back across the iron bridge to join them on the towpath. She led them past Zilombo's den. Mizz Z had said it was safe. But Jin's heart was thumping. He half expected to hear the warlike shake of that ankle bracelet. But there were no chinking bottle tops. No sound from the den at all.

Frankie retrieved her red spray can on the way. Even fear of Zilombo couldn't make her forget it. Spray cans were very expensive to buy. But this one had been a real bargain—a giant-sized can she'd bought at a knockdown price from a market stall.

"Here, hold Smiler," she said, passing a wriggling baby to Jin.

Then she stashed the bargain can in a secret pocket she'd sewn specially in her skirt. As Mizz Z had noticed, Frankie liked to customize her clothes.

Frankie also had her key in that secret pocket—the one to the back door of the factory. She let them in, then locked it behind them.

Jin staggered up the endless steps, lugging Smiler. He suddenly felt really weary. It had been a long, traumatic day. And it was only teatime. He was rehearsing in his mind what he would say to Mum and his grandparents. Mizz Z would be hard enough to explain. But what about Zilombo? Jin couldn't imagine how he'd even start.

But when Jin burst through the flat door, yelling, "It's me!" there was no answering call.

"They're still out," said Frankie, checking in all the rooms. She shoved aside some bamboo hoops and a dragon's head, then slumped on the huge sagging sofa.

"Hmmm," murmured Mizz Z approvingly, inspecting the heavy oak door to the flat. "That is a stout door. Like the one downstairs. Even Zilombo might have problems breaking this down. Does it lock?"

"I think it does," said Frankie from the sofa. "But Gran and Grandad never bother."

"Well, perhaps we should," said Mizz Z.

"Why? I thought you said Zilombo wouldn't come

up here?" said Jin, feeling frantic again, just when he'd started to calm down.

"In my professional opinion, she won't," said Mizz Z in her brisk, businesslike chief inspector's voice. "I am just taking precautions, that's all. Zilombo is a very ancient creature, from lakes and swamps. She won't enter buildings unless she has to. No more than a dinosaur would. Or a crocodile."

Jin nodded, half-reassured. "Hope you're right," he said.

Mizz Z replied, "I am almost always right." She wasn't boasting; it was just a fact of life.

Frankie told Mizz Z, "Grandma and Grandad Tang got a letter about demolishing this building. Mum's taken them to Citizens Advice."

A sudden thought struck Jin. "What about when they come back? Shouldn't we warn them about Zilombo? Frankie can ring them on her mobile."

"Which way do they enter the building?" asked Mizz Z.

"Through the front door," said Frankie, "where Mum parks her car."

"Then even if Zilombo is awake and back guarding her den, she will not see them?"

"No," said Frankie.

"Then we need not tell them. Not yet."

"Aren't you going to tell *anyone*?" asked Jin. "What about the police?"

"Especially not them," said Mizz Z. "It is not their business. And my job is secret, remember? I am undercover. And why spread panic when we do not need to? I will deal with Zilombo," Mizz Z assured them, her chin tilting defiantly. "She will soon be back inside her mudball. And no one here need even know she escaped."

Jin gave Smiler a Jammy Dodger biscuit. He mashed it into his mouth with both fists, then— spraying crumbs—he crawled off to play with a basket of dragon eyeballs stored behind the sofa.

"Want a cold drink, Mizz Z?" asked Frankie, leaping up from among the cushions. She dashed off into the kitchen. Jin heard her yank the fridge door open. He had never known Frankie to be so obliging before. Mizz Z seemed to have somehow broken through that spiky shell that Frankie liked to surround herself with.

"Your grandparents make dancing dragons?" asked Mizz Z, gazing round at the clutter of bits of dragon, bamboo hoops, and bales of glittering fabric. "This is how they make their living?"

Jin nodded. "My Grandad Tang used to be a dragon dancer," he told Mizz Z. Jin was surprised he came out with that fact. Grandad Tang hadn't dragon danced for ages. He'd told Jin once: "It's a young man's game! Holding those poles high. Making the dragon twist and turn above you. It needs a lot of strength and control."

Jin had instantly decided, "I wouldn't be able to do it, then." Controlling a long, writhing Chinese dragon, held above him on poles, seemed impossible to him.

Mizz Z went over to the window and stroked the crimson-and-gold dragon's crested spine. She nodded her approval. "He is a very fine fellow. He's finished, isn't he?"

"Yeah," said Jin. "He's all ready to dance. He's

only a two-person dragon. It takes lots of dancers to work the really big ones."

"Nevertheless, he looks very fierce. But why does he have a mirror here?" asked Mizz Z. She pointed to a small round mirror that glittered, like a third eye, in the center of the dragon's forehead.

"It's supposed to help him chase away monsters. That's what Grandad Tang said. Monsters see themselves in that mirror and think, 'Help! A scary monster!' And they run for their lives."

"Oh, really?" said Mizz Z.

"Grandad says monsters are dumb. They've got to be, haven't they, to be scared by their own reflection? Anyhoo, it's not *true*," added Jin. "It's just an old Chinese story."

Mizz Z seemed faraway. So lost in thought, she forgot to correct Jin for saying *anyhoo*. "Some of these old stories are truer than you think," she murmured.

But Jin didn't want to talk about old stories. When he was a little kid, he'd adored hearing those tales, sitting on Grandad Tang's knee. But now that he was older, he never thought about them. They seemed quaint and old-fashioned, nothing to do with his life now. Like something stored, forgotten, at the back of a dusty cupboard.

What Jin wanted was a reply to a question. The one he'd asked Mizz Z before but she'd never answered.

"Mizz Z, did Zilombo scoff your baby brother?"

CHAPTER
NINE

For a moment, Mizz Z didn't reply. And Jin thought, *Oh no, I've been rude again.* When would he learn not to open his mouth and stick his foot in it?

But Mizz Z didn't seem in the least upset. Or if she was, she didn't show it. Instead, she came over to the sofa, sat down, and said calmly, "Now where did I leave off my story?"

Jin sat cross-legged on the rug to listen. "Your baby brother was toddling toward the lake kicking the mudball," he reminded her eagerly.

"You have a very good memory," said Mizz Z.

Jin couldn't help a tiny flicker of pride. He did

have a fantastic memory. Mum said it was an upside of being dyspraxic. When you can't write down what the teacher says fast enough, you have to store it all in your mind instead.

"You said you heard his Fanta bottle-top necklace jangling," Jin added.

"Ah, yes," said Mizz Z. She was staring dreamily into space, as if Jin didn't exist. But then she started to speak again.

"When I realized my brother was gone," said Mizz Z, "I ran after him, calling his name. I yelled, with all the power of my lungs, 'Kapito, where are you?' And I heard him wail, 'I kicked my football into the lake!'"

Frankie came in, balancing three glasses on a tray. Silently she put a drink down beside Mizz Z. Mizz Z didn't even notice. Carefully, so she didn't distract Mizz Z, Frankie knelt down on the rug beside Jin, with her biker boots tucked beneath her and her black funereal skirts spread around her like ravens' wings.

"I searched the shore of the lake," Mizz Z was

saying, "all through the reed beds. But I could not find Kapito anywhere. Then something came plopping up to the lake surface. It was the mudball, broken in half and empty. I have never been so afraid in my life. Because suddenly I remembered that old story of Zilombo. How she could survive for years inside a mudball, but hatch out when it got wet. And how she sometimes took children for her food store. And kept them in her den."

Jin couldn't stand the suspense. "So did she eat Kapito then?"

Mizz Z didn't even hear him. "There was no time to get help," she continued. "And part of me thought, *That stupid old story cannot be true. It is just to frighten children.* But, all the same, Kapito was missing. So I dived into the water, down, down. I did not see Zilombo. But I found my brother. It was a miracle he was still alive . . ."

This time Jin couldn't smother his questions. They just came tumbling out: "What? Underwater? Why hadn't he drowned?"

Mizz Z turned to stare at him.

"Sorry! I'll shut up, I swear!" said Jin hastily. But, to his surprise, Mizz Z paused to answer his questions.

"As I have mentioned before," she explained, "Zilombo likes her food fresh. So she had chosen her den carefully. This den had a big bubble of air in it, to keep her food alive."

Jin forgot that two seconds ago he'd sworn to keep quiet. He asked, "Why couldn't Kapito swim out?"

"Zilombo had wedged him between tree roots. But she made sure his head was inside that bubble of air. So Kapito could still breathe. But he was stuck fast."

Frankie shot Jin a look that said: "Will you stop interrupting!"

Jin slapped both hands over his mouth so those questions that were flapping like birds inside his skull couldn't fly out. He thought instead about Kapito, trapped in his underwater prison, just waiting for Zilombo to get hungry. It could be in two minutes, or two hours, or two days. What terrors would be in *his* mind? Jin was good at guessing other people's feelings. But this time, he couldn't even *begin* to imagine.

Mizz Z turned her gaze into space, once again under the spell of her story. "I pulled Kapito free. I told him, 'Kapito, take a big gulp of air!' I did too. Then we left the air bubble. I swam for the surface, with Kapito clinging round my neck. Then Zilombo struck! She had been deep down in the lake, fishing for eels. Kapito let go of my neck. Zilombo came after me. I saw her great teeth. Her nails were like spears! I thought I would die. I opened my mouth to cry out but water went in . . ."

This time it was Frankie who couldn't bear the suspense. "How did you escape?" she cried out. "What happened to Kapito?"

Mizz Z turned to gaze at them both. Her face was grim, haunted by memories. "We were both very lucky," she said. "I did not know it, but my dad was on the lake in his canoe, fishing for *chambo*. He saw Kapito pop up to the surface, hauled him in. Kapito could only scream one word: 'Zilombo!' At first my dad did not believe it. But Kapito kept screaming and pointing into the water: 'Zilombo! Zilombo!' Then my dad looked down. He saw me, struggling in Zilombo's grasp. He acted swiftly. He tipped his whole day's catch of *chambo* into the lake. When Zilombo saw the free food, she stabbed at it and not me. In those few moments I escaped and my dad pulled me, half-drowned, into his canoe. Then he paddled like crazy for the shore."

"Wow! So you were both OK," said Jin.

"We were not OK yet," Mizz Z corrected him. "Our house was on the lakeshore, near Zilombo's den. Zilombo can run as fast as a croc on dry land. We got there just before her and barricaded the door. But Zilombo leaped onto our roof. You know how springy her legs are?"

Jin nodded, shuddering.

"She began raking holes in our roof," Mizz Z continued. "She reached in, trying to stab us with her nails. Dad said, 'Quick, hide under the bed.' But I was not quick enough to hide, and that was when she jabbed my face and I was blinded in one eye.

"My brother screamed. And my mum, she was

trying to quiet him, singing a lullaby. But as Mum sang, a strange thing happened. My brother didn't calm down, but Zilombo did. She fell asleep! She sprawled on our roof, snoring, with her arms dangling through the holes she'd made.

"My dad told my mum, 'Keep singing!'

"Then Dad crawled out from under the bed and grabbed Mum's dress-making shears. He sliced through Zilombo's fingernails, one by one. Chop, chop, chop," said Mizz Z, miming the actions.

"Her fingernails?" frowned Frankie, staring at her own long, black glossy talons. "Why did he do that?"

"Because that is where her power lies," said Mizz Z as if it was obvious.

"Oh right," said Frankie. "So what happened next?"

"It was amazing!" said Mizz Z. "At the last snip, Zilombo woke up. When she saw her fingernails were missing, she started howling with grief. She slid off our roof and ran screeching away! Dad took me to the hospital on his bike. And afterward when I was getting better, I asked Dad, "How did you know to chop off her fingernails?"

"My dad answered, 'Because I remember the old stories. Two things make Zilombo return to a mudball, so the old stories say. One is drought. And the other is to cut her fingernails. When you chop them off she loses her strength. She hides away in a mudball. Inside the mudball the nails slowly grow back. Then as soon as the ball gets wet, Zilombo hatches again, stronger than ever.'"

"But did the old stories say anything about that lullaby putting her to sleep?" asked Jin.

"No," said Mizz Z. "We found that out by accident. But Zilombo is always changing. I wasn't sure whether it would work again."

"But it did!" said Frankie. "So does that mean you can put her to sleep whenever you like?"

"Maybe," said Mizz Z doubtfully. "We shall see." She took a sip of her drink. For the first time Jin heard a metro train rattling over the factory. They sped by every few minutes, shaking the windows. But during Mizz Z's story, he hadn't even noticed.

"Wait a minute," said Frankie suddenly. "You

haven't finished your story. Zilombo's back in a mudball? Right? After your dad chopped off her fingernails? But how did the mudball get here to England? How did it end up on top of Madalitso's wardrobe?"

"Madalitso lived in England even then," said Mizz Z. "But she had been born in our village. Later, my dad went out looking for Zilombo. He found her mudball. So he posted it to Madalitso here in England. He just wanted to send Zilombo far, far away from our lake. And England seemed to him as distant as the moon. Madalitso promised to keep the ball away from water so Zilombo could never again take any more children. And she kept her promise for twenty years."

"Did you say, your dad *posted* the mudball?" Jin interrupted. "You mean, like, in a *parcel*?"

"That is what I said," agreed Mizz Z. "He sent her air mail."

"That's a bit risky if you ask me!" said Jin. "What if she'd gotten wet? Hatched out inside the plane? Just imagine the panic!"

"My dad carved warnings on the mudball," Mizz Z pointed out.

"Yeah, in Chewa!" protested Jin.

Now her tale was almost done, Mizz Z was back to her usual, fiery self. "Well, what do you expect?" she fired at Jin. "My dad did not speak English! But I learned English at school," Mizz Z explained. "I was top of my class! So I wrote Madalitso's address on the parcel. I marked it: HANDLE WITH CARE."

Mizz Z had one last thing to reveal. "After the mudball incident," she told them, "it became my ambition to one day join RAAAA, which takes care of ancient artifacts worldwide. And I ended up in the most secret branch of the agency. Inspecting high-risk artifacts here in your country."

"But I don't understand," said Jin. "How did all these artifacts end up here in England? Surely they weren't all sent by air mail?"

"Not most of them," confirmed Mizz Z. "Many were stolen, centuries ago, from museums and private collections."

"Why don't the countries they were stolen from

ask for them back?" asked Frankie.

"Well, they do, all the time," said Mizz Z. "They just keep quiet about the ones they *don't* want. Monsters rampaging about, and curses and magic from ancient times, can be very inconvenient."

"Isn't it a bit, like, irresponsible," asked Frankie, shrugging, "to leave all these dangerous ancient artifacts somewhere else? Like here, for instance?"

"Then they shouldn't have been stolen in the first place!" said Mizz Z. "And I think RAAAA is being very responsible. We could just leave those countries to cope with the consequences. But that wouldn't be right. So RAAAA sends its inspectors all over the world, to make sure there is no risk."

"But what about Zilombo?" asked Jin.

"Sometimes accidents happen," said Mizz Z coolly. "But don't worry, as I told you, I will get Zilombo safely back in a mudball. I will do it tonight. One way or another."

Then Frankie spoke up again. "When your dad found Zilombo in a mudball, you know, after he chopped her fingernails, why didn't he kill her? After all, she'd tried to kill you and Kapito."

"Yeah," agreed Jin. "Your dad could have done it easy-peasy. Zilombo couldn't hurt him, trapped inside that ball. Why didn't he smash the mudball up, with her inside it? Like burn it or something? Get rid of her forever."

Mizz Z looked outraged. Her bronze bangles jangled angrily as she answered, "My dad is not a murderer! Besides, Zilombo cannot help her behavior. *She is what she is.* We must learn to live with such wild creatures, as we do with lions or snakes. Are you suggesting she should be destroyed?"

Jin didn't know anymore what he was suggesting. Mizz Z had a way of tying your mind in knots. But then he heard the front door to the factory creak open downstairs. *Zilombo!* he thought, his blood freezing in his veins. Until he realized that whoever it was had let themselves in with a key.

"It must be Mum and Grandma and Grandad Tang coming back," he told Mizz Z.

"So what do we tell them about *you*?" asked Frankie, frowning.

"*Not* that I am chief inspector," declared Mizz Z. "No one must know of my real importance. I shall pretend I am just an ordinary person."

Smiler was fed up of playing with eyeballs. He'd moved onto a basket of gongs, drums, and cymbals that was also stored behind the sofa. They made the wild music for the Chinese dragon dance. Smiler picked up two cymbals and bashed them together with an ear-splitting *CLASH!!* A look of startled joy spread across his face, as if to say, "Did I make that brilliant sound?" He clashed the cymbals again, even louder, just to make sure.

Mizz Z turned her elegant, swanlike neck to gaze down at Smiler. "You are a very noisy baby," she told him. Smiler gave her a drooly grin.

The flat door was pushed open. Grandad Tang came in first.

Smiler poked his head from behind the sofa. At the sight of Grandad Tang's kindly face, Smiler chucked down the cymbals and squealed a joyful greeting. He went crawling over at a fast gallop and Grandad Tang swung him up.

Mum and Grandma Tang came in next.

Mizz Z rose to her feet. She towered over Jin's tiny mum. "A. J. Zauyamakanda," she said briskly, stooping to shake Mum by the hand. "Hello, pleased to meet you," she said in Mandarin.

Frankie's eyes widened in amazement. "Did you know Mizz Z spoke Mandarin?" she whispered to Jin.

Jin shook his head wonderingly and whispered back, "No, I told her Mum and Granny and Grandad did. But I never knew that she did!"

There was one thing, though, that he did know. Mizz Z was *full* of surprises.

Meanwhile, as Mizz Z had predicted, Zilombo had woken up and squeezed, ratlike, back to the Oozeburn end of her den.

The tide was still high. The water was only a meter or so below her den. With one webbed foot, Zilombo fished in the scummy waves and pulled up a shopping cart.

"Ugh?"

That wasn't what she wanted. She chucked it back. She fished once more and, on one hooked, yellow toenail, hauled up the grid she'd booted out. She rammed it back in place so she had a front door again.

Now she squatted in the pipe mouth, peering out through the grid with greedy green eyes. She was millions of years old. She had seen dinosaurs, woolly mammoths, saber-toothed tigers, Neanderthals. All of them, or rather their babies, had been her prey, at one time or another.

But this time, no prey, no young gazelles or baby wildebeest, came down to the banks of the Oozeburn to drink. She searched the folds of her slimy gray skin for scuttling crabs to eat, crunched them between her fangs like popcorn.

Bored with that, she rasped the flesh off a dead fish with her rough, furry tongue. She used its backbone to comb her matted orange mane. Then she did a strange thing. She sprinkled her long hair with fish scales that glittered like sequins. She ran a strand through her claws and gave a satisfied croak, as if she was pleased with how pretty it looked.

A noise farther down the pipe made her shark eyes gleam.

Had her food store come back? She twisted her great bulky body round to look.

She peered hopefully into the dark, her snout sniffing the air for his smell. But no food store came crawling back to see her.

A deep sigh rumbled up from her belly. She quite missed having him around. It was lonely being Zilombo. She would never find a mate. She was unique, ever changing. There wasn't another creature like her on Earth.

She sighed again, like wind through a graveyard.

If Smiler did come crawling back she'd have a choice: whether to scoff him, or keep him for company. Only there might be no choice at all. Zilombo had *some* human feelings; Jin had seen it in her face. But she was still mostly beast. And if her beastly instincts took over, Smiler would be next on her dinner menu. She just wouldn't be able to help herself.

A harsh grating sound, like the whine of a buzz

saw, came from Zilombo's throat. She rocked herself to and fro and stamped softly. To the jingling rhythm of her ankle bracelet, she began crooning an ancient Malawian lullaby to comfort herself.

Tied to her ankle bracelet was a red shoelace. Zilombo had found it alongside the shredded remains of Smiler's baby boot when she was crawling back through the pipe. She raised her foot to her nose and sniffed the shoelace.

"Mmmmm," she murmured, sniffing again. The expression in her tiny green eyes, flickering beneath that jutting brow, was hard to read. It seemed to be hunger. But for what? For company, or for her next meal?

Then suddenly she stopped rocking and crooning. Her fingers were buzzing.

"Ugh?" she said, holding up a scaly, webbed hand. A tiny electric spark jumped between two of her fingers. She put her hand to the grid in front of her. An electric charge shot into it, fizzed around the metal, until the whole grid burned with blue fire. "Aha!" croaked Zilombo.

A thought was forming slowly in her brain. She'd seen this kind of thing before: stingrays and eels that could stun and even kill their prey with electric shocks. And now she, Zilombo, could do it too! Every hatching made her more powerful, gave her new and more spectacular hunting skills. This time, it was a collapsible skeleton and stingray hands. A few more hatchings out and she'd be the perfect predator. No living thing would escape her.

Zilombo stared, entranced, at her own hands fizzing like fireworks.

She could control it too, turn the current off when she chose, just like switching off a light. She turned her electricity off, then on again, off and on, off and on.

"Aha!" she croaked again in triumph. She couldn't wait to try out her new weapon.

An unfortunate rat chose that very instant to squeeze through the grid. *Ssst!* Zilombo sizzled him. The rat felt no pain; he never even knew what had hit him.

Zilombo picked him up. He was very crunchy: it

was like eating a big, rat-flavored crisp. "Mmmm," she said, licking her thin lips, thinking of fried *chambo*.

Then Zilombo threw back her shaggy head. A dreadful din, like herons squawking, echoed off the metal walls of her den. She held her shaking belly. Zilombo was having a good laugh.

CHAPTER
TEN

Five stories above Zilombo, on the top floor of the old factory, Jin was standing beside the dancing dragon, staring out of the window of Grandma and Grandad Tang's flat.

A metro train came speeding across the city skyline, its silver sides flashing pink in the setting sun.

It came closer, closer, until it seemed it would crash into the flat. Then at the last minute it soared away on its high rail line that went right over the factory chimneys.

"Would you like another Jammy Dodger?"

Grandma Tang asked Mizz Z.

"Thank you so very much," said Mizz Z in Mandarin, graciously taking a biscuit.

Jin's grandparents smiled in approval. Like Mizz Z, they were very big on manners.

Wow, they're getting on really well, thought Jin, relieved.

At first, Jin's mum and grandparents had been wary of Mizz Z. It's not every day you meet such a tall, proud, part pirate, part warrior princess. But Mizz Z had used all of her charm on them. Speaking some Mandarin was a big help. Now they were nattering away in English like old friends, talking about Madalitso's accident and Grandma Tang's shock when they'd gotten the letter about the factory being demolished.

But not one word escaped Mizz Z's lips about Zilombo, that ticking time bomb, squatting down in her den. Jin was thinking, *Mizz Z said she'd deal with her tonight.* And it was already getting dark.

Frankie came creeping up to stand by his side. They stole anxious glances at each other. Frankie whispered, "Wonder how Mizz Z's planning to do it? Get Zilombo back in a mudball, I mean."

They soon had their answer. Mizz Z finished her Jammy Dodger. She rose, tall and dignified, a tower of jazzy colors, from the sofa she shared with a Chinese dragon.

"I must go now," she announced.

"Are you going to see Madalitso in the hospital?" asked Mum.

"Later I will do that." Mizz Z nodded. "But I have something rather important I must do first." She turned to Grandad Tang, who'd been sitting bouncing Smiler on his knee, singing him old Chinese nursery rhymes. "I would be very grateful," said Mizz Z, with her most dazzling smile, "if you would lend me a very strong, sharp pair of scissors."

Grandad didn't ask why. He was a serene, philosophical guy. And anyhow, Mizz Z wasn't the kind of person you questioned. Grandad padded in his slippers about the flat, disappearing into different rooms. He came back with a choice of shears that the Tangs used for making Chinese dragons.

"These will cut through bamboo," said Grandad. "Or even metal."

"Perfect," said Mizz Z, selecting a wicked-looking pair whose blades had sharp little teeth like a saw. She swept toward the flat door. "It was a pleasure to meet you," she told Jin's mum and the Tangs. Then she let herself out of the flat.

Frankie and Jin gaped for a second. Frankie was the first to move. She went sprinting after Mizz Z. Jin went lurching off too. "Back in a sec, Mum," he threw over his shoulder.

They caught up with Mizz Z on a cold empty landing two floors down. "Oh, there you are," she said, as if she'd been expecting them to follow.

"You're going to cut her nails, aren't you?" said Jin.

"Of course," answered Mizz Z calmly. "Zilombo's nails are her Achilles heel."

"What?" said Jin, baffled.

"Do you not know these old stories?" asked Mizz Z severely. "What do they teach you in school?" Then she explained. "Like Zilombo, the great Greek warrior,

Achilles, had one weakness. As a baby, his mum dipped him in the sacred river Styx so that no weapons could pierce his skin. But she forgot that she was holding him by his heel. And that is where an arrow killed him."

Frankie was fidgeting restlessly, unraveling frills from her black party frock. As soon as Mizz Z finished speaking, words burst out of her mouth. "Let us come with you! We rescued Smiler together, didn't we? We make a great team, the three of us!"

For a moment, Mizz Z's rather fierce, hawklike features softened. "I must admit," she said, "that you children have spirit. Even if you do not know the old stories. Or Chewa."

"I know the old Chinese stories," protested Jin. "Grandad Tang told me!"

"Ah, yes," said Mizz Z, nodding her approval. "I forgot."

Jin slapped his palm against his forehead. Why was he babbling about Chinese stories? That wasn't what he meant to say at all. "Let us come with you," he blurted out. Normally he wouldn't have offered his help. But there was something about Mizz Z that made Jin believe in himself, forget his own clumsiness. With her, he could do amazing things.

So he was crushed by disappointment when Mizz Z said firmly, "I cannot allow it. I alone must run the risks. Besides, it is no big deal."

"But—" interrupted Frankie.

"No," said Mizz Z, silencing her with an amber stare. "I need you both to stay here with your mother and grandparents. To make sure that they do not leave this building, especially by the back door. It will not be safe for anyone to be down near Zilombo's den tonight."

"But you're going down there!" protested Jin. "Aren't you?"

"Yes, but I am the chief inspector," Mizz Z told him, as if that settled the matter. Then she sternly commanded them both, "Do not go outside tonight, no matter what you hear or see." She repeated, "*No matter what you hear or see.* Do you understand?"

"Yeah, we understand, don't we, Jin?" said Frankie. Once again, Jin was amazed at how respectful Frankie was being. She didn't kick up a fuss, like she usually would. Or rage: "Nobody tells *me* what to do!"

"Can I borrow your back door key?" Mizz Z asked Frankie.

Frankie turned her back and rummaged in her secret pocket. She didn't like anyone knowing where she kept her spray can. She turned round again and handed the key to Mizz Z.

"I shall return before you know it," said Mizz Z. Then she paused a moment. "Actually," she said, "I think I shall leave my backpack here. I don't want my laptop damaged." She unslung her backpack and gave it to Frankie.

"I'll look after it," Frankie promised.

Mizz Z hesitated for a few more seconds. "But if by any chance I do not return," she told Frankie, "make sure you inform RAAAA immediately. You will find their contact details on my laptop."

"But you will come back, won't you?" asked Jin, his face twisted up with distress.

"Of course I will," said Mizz Z briskly. "I am just taking precautions."

Then Mizz Z strode away, upright and haughty as ever, down the stairs. First her orange and red head wrap was lost to view. Then the smack of her flip-flops faded. The back door to the factory slammed. And she was gone. It was as if a force of nature, a volcano or a whirlwind, had left the building.

Frankie and Jin were left behind on the bare, chilly landing, staring helplessly at each other.

Then they both started trudging back upstairs.

In the Tangs' flat, Frankie said, "Grandma, can I stay again tonight?"

And Jin added, "Can I too?"

"Of course," said Grandma Tang, pleased. "You can cheer us up, me and Grandad. After that letter. And what they said at Citizens Advice."

"They said," Mum explained, "that this building is a safety hazard. That it's definitely going to be demolished. It's dreadful. Losing their home at their age!" She got up. "It's time to take Smiler home. Think I'll pop in to see Madalitso in the hospital on my way."

"Leave Smiler here too," said Grandma Tang. "We

love having him to stay."

"Are you sure?" asked Mum. "That would be great."

But Frankie muttered, "He'd be safer at home."

Mum didn't know anything about Zilombo and the traumatic events of that morning when Smiler had been snatched for Zilombo's food store. So she thought Frankie was just causing trouble. "What are you talking about?" she asked her daughter.

"Are you saying Grandad and me can't look after him?" said Grandma, looking hurt and bewildered.

Frankie said, "No, I didn't say that! Oh, forget it," she scowled, hurling herself on the sofa.

Grandad Tang, always the peacemaker, told Mum, "You'd better go, or you'll miss visiting time."

"You going out the front door, Mum?" asked Jin, trying to make it seem like a casual question.

But Mum was immediately suspicious. "Course I am," she said. "My car's parked out there. Why do you want to know?"

"Oh, no reason, it's not important," shrugged Jin, turning away. He was rubbish at telling lies. Every emotion he had always showed in his face.

Mum finally left, but not before shooting a warning glare at Frankie, as if to say: "Behave yourself! Don't you dare go upsetting Grandma again!"

"Huh!" said Frankie, tossing her chin defiantly.

It was the story of her life, being misunderstood. She felt like dashing out, to spray paint her tag somewhere, like she always did in times of stress. But then she remembered her promise to Mizz Z. She had to stay here, make sure that Grandma and Grandad stayed in the flat and didn't go down to the Oozeburn. And now there was Smiler to worry about too. So she resorted to her second favorite method of letting off steam. She clambered over the sofa to reach the basket of Chinese instruments. She picked up a drum that looked like a big tambourine and beat out a wild, frenzied tune on it with a wooden stick.

Grandma and Grandad Tang smiled and clapped along. Grandad even did a few swirling moves from his dragon-dancing days.

After a few minutes of demented bashing, Frankie put the drum back in the basket. Calmer now, she climbed back to her seat on the sofa and, hugging Mizz Z's backpack to keep it safe, slumped among the cushions.

Grandma and Grandad Tang went into the kitchen to make dinner. It was Saturday, so it was cabbage and chicken, steamed dumplings, and sticky rice. They took Smiler with them.

"What happened to your shoe, Smiler?" Jin and Frankie heard Grandad chuckle. "You've lost it somewhere."

"I'm scared for Mizz Z," said Jin, thinking about the telltale flutter below Mizz Z's eye patch.

"Don't talk like that!" said Frankie scornfully. "That's stupid! She said it was no big deal, remember?"

But they both rushed over to the window. It was dark now. The city was a maze of blurred, twinkling lights. But the Oozeburn and its banks were unlit. Why light up a weedy wasteland where no one ever goes? When Frankie and Jin gazed down it was like looking into a murky pit.

"Open the window," said Frankie. The factory

windows were long; they reached almost to the floor. "Then maybe we'll be able to hear something."

But all they could hear was the growl of city traffic on the overpass and the rattle of some distant metro train. Beside them, the dancing dragon's silver fringes blew softly in the night breeze. The mirror on his forehead, meant to scare monsters with their own reflection, gleamed in the moonlight like a ghostly eye.

"What's going on down there?" fretted Jin.

Without even knowing she was doing it, Frankie began chewing her black glossy nails.

Neither of them noticed either that Smiler, bored with watching Grandma and Grandad Tang make dumplings, had come crawling out of the kitchen.

He used the door frame to pull himself up then took two wobbly steps forward. He was walking! With a look of wonder on his face, he began staggering across the room, toward the open window.

Far below them, Mizz Z tucked the back door key to the factory into the folds of her head wrap.

Then she crept, stealthy as a panther, toward Zilombo's den. It wasn't as dark down here as it appeared from above. Especially when the moon slid out from behind the clouds and spilled its silvery light right down into the Oozeburn's deep channel.

As chief inspector for RAAAA, Mizz Z had dealt with many cases where, due to unforeseen circumstances, artifacts had been reactivated, regained their ancient powers. But she had handled each case with brisk efficiency, quickly made each artifact harmless again. And it had all been done in secret. No one, not the owners of the artifacts, nor the museums where they were stored, had ever found out they had been in danger.

But Zilombo was different. Mizz Z liked to be in control. But somehow she didn't feel in control of this case. For a start, three children had been involved: Jin, Frankie, and Smiler. That made things much more complicated. And secondly, this case was personal. Zilombo had kidnapped her little brother and half blinded Mizz Z. It's hard to forget things like that.

"You must!" Mizz Z hissed fiercely to herself. She

didn't want her emotions to cloud her judgment. That way you made mistakes.

Mizz Z had a plan, of course. It was very simple. Almost too simple. There were just two parts to it.

Part 1: Put Zilombo to sleep with a lullaby.
Part 2: Chop off her fingernails.

Then Zilombo would immediately lose her power, shrink, and make a fresh mudball around herself. She'd be harmless again, imprisoned, hopefully forever. Panic over. Job done.

It had worked all those years ago, after Zilombo had snatched Kapito.

"Why shouldn't it work again?" Mizz Z tried to reassure herself. And she'd given the lullaby part of the plan a trial run already—Zilombo had fallen asleep like a baby. So what could possibly go wrong?

If only that nagging doubt would stop tormenting her: *Never underestimate Zilombo.*

Mizz Z was crouching on the towpath now, just across from Zilombo's den in the old sewer pipe.

Carefully Mizz Z slid off her bronze bracelets so they didn't clash and give her away. She left them hanging on a bramble bush.

She tried to keep her mind clear. But the smell of the den—stinking fish and rotting rat—drifted up. Mizz Z had a flashback to that crocodile's den all those years ago.

The den Zilombo had taken over after she'd hatched.

The den where Zilombo had taken Kapito.

There had been putrid meat in there too. Mizz Z had smelled it in the air bubble. She had touched it—a slimy, oozing antelope leg—when she was frantically trying to free Kapito.

"Stop it!" Mizz Z ordered herself, forcing her mind back to the present.

Suddenly she caught a whiff of a new, unfamiliar smell. *Burnt barbecue?* she thought. But she had no time to wonder about that now.

"Just get on with it," she told herself severely. This case had already taken up too much time. She had other artifacts to inspect in this city—the next on her laptop files was a tribal mask.

Mizz Z grasped the big shears she'd borrowed from the Tangs. She crept over the iron bridge to the other side of the Oozeburn. Now she was just above Zilombo's den, staring down at it.

"Zilombo!" she shouted down.

"Ugh?" croaked Zilombo, who'd already smelled her coming. Under her jutting brow, her little eyes gleamed shiftily. Her ankle bracelet rattled a warning. With one mighty kick, she booted out her front door, then craned her neck upward.

Mizz Z found herself staring down at a dog's muzzle and a croc's wolfish, snaggle-toothed grin. She felt an unexpected jolt of fear, as if she'd become a little, frightened girl again. Then she got a grip and put Part One of her plan into action.

Mizz Z started crooning that ancient lullaby, the one her mum had sung to her. The same one mums in her village had sung to their babies for generations. Mizz Z's voice was a low hum, like the drowsy murmur of bees. Dreamy enough to coax the wildest beast into a doze. Especially a beast like Zilombo who, with that part of her that was human, sometimes longed for a mother's love.

And it seemed, at first, to work like a charm. Just like it had before.

Zilombo's shaggy head flopped. She slumped back into the pipe. Soon, her snoring echoed along the Oozeburn.

Mizz Z got ready to climb the ladder down the brick wall to the den entrance.

But Mizz Z didn't know that inside the pipe, under those craggy brows, Zilombo's eyes weren't closed. Through narrow slits, they gleamed with cunning. Mizz Z didn't know either that, at this moment, Zilombo's predator's instincts were in total control. That even singing lullabies couldn't tame her.

Because Zilombo was too thrilled by her new weapon. Even now, she was playing games with it. *Sssst!* She made blue sparks crackle between her fingers. She'd already zapped the rat. But she couldn't wait to try it out on bigger prey.

Zilombo started a bloodthirsty chuckle. Then she remembered she was pretending to be asleep and changed it into a snore that reverberated, like a drum roll, along the metal pipe.

Is she really asleep? thought Mizz Z, hesitating. She thought she'd detected a different sound. But when the snores came again, she began descending the ladder.

Halfway down, she swung across into the pipe entrance and crouched, facing the beast.

Mizz Z hadn't been this close to Zilombo for ages, not since that struggle many years ago in the lake. She breathed in Zilombo's dead-crab perfume and that burnt-barbecue smell she couldn't identify. She saw the gray shrimps scuttling in the damp folds of Zilombo's baggy gray elephant skin.

"Zilombo?" she whispered.

Zilombo twitched like a dog in her sleep. Her swivel eyes, just visible in the gloom, were rolled up to show the whites.

She's dead to the world, thought Mizz Z. Deep in dreamland. She took several deep breaths to give herself courage, then reached out to lift one of Zilombo's great webbed hands that lay limply on her knees.

Mizz Z couldn't help shuddering at the sight of the brutal talons that had blinded her. They seemed hornier and thicker than they'd been twenty years ago. That was no big surprise. Everything else about Zilombo had grown tougher, more deadly, since her last hatching. So perhaps her nails had as well.

But the shears Mizz Z was holding should slice through them easily. Hadn't Grandad Tang said they could cut through metal?

Still Mizz Z hesitated, seized by doubts. She drew back her own hand for a second.

Zilombo snored again. Her bulldog jowls wobbled. Her snake lips writhed, as if, in her sleep, she was smiling at some private joke.

Then: "You are cowardly as a jackal!" Mizz Z mocked herself. "Just cut her nails, A. J. Zauyama-kanda!" So Mizz Z reached out again for that slimy paw.

She tried to saw through the nails. But the shears wouldn't cut through them; they didn't even leave a scratch! *Her nails are harder than metal!* thought Mizz Z. *They are as hard as diamonds. These shears are useless!* She threw them aside.

And that was her last action, because Zilombo switched on her secret weapon. A bolt of electricity shot from Zilombo's fingers into Mizz Z's body. Mizz Z crashed sideways into the wall of the pipe.

Zilombo sprang back in a great kangaroo leap as Mizz Z's body jerked straight, shook with spasms for a few seconds, then lay very, very still.

There was a smell of burning in the pipe.

"Aha!" croaked Zilombo in triumph. She felt very clever. She'd never caught a human as big as this before.

Her predator's instincts pulled her two ways. One was to keep this prize in her food store—it was empty since Smiler had been stolen. The other was to scoff her prey now and have a huge feast, fill her belly to bursting, like lions do after a kill.

"Mmmm," mused Zilombo, scratching at an itchy place on her scaly ankle. She pulled back her lips in a snarl to show savage croc fangs. She crawled forward, sniffing all around Mizz Z's unmoving body.

Suddenly howls floated down from high above.

Zilombo might be short-sighted. But her hearing, like her sense of smell, was wolf keen. And just as wolves can recognize the howls of other wolves, Zilombo knew exactly who these howls belonged to.

Zilombo snarled softly with excitement.

She trampled over Mizz Z's body to reach the mouth of the pipe. The tide had gone out again; there was no water in the Oozeburn. Zilombo sprang down into smelly mud. She stared upward. She could just make out bright, shining lights on the top floor of the factory. That was where the howls were coming from.

Zilombo raised her face to the moon and stars. She threw back her shaggy mane, opened her jaws, and howled back, as if to say: "I'm coming!"

CHAPTER
ELEVEN

Up in Grandma and Grandad Tang's flat, Jin had turned round to see Smiler, his arms and legs jerking like a mad puppet, wobbling toward the open window, unable to stop himself.

It took a few seconds to register—*he's walking!*—and Smiler had almost pitched headlong through the window before Jin snatched him up. His heart thumping at what might have happened, Jin crushed Smiler to him.

"Smiler, you nearly gave me a heart attack. You almost fell out that window!"

Smiler howled with frustration, because he wanted

to be put down again to try out his new walking skills.

Grandma and Grandad Tang had come rushing in from the kitchen, Grandad still clutching his bamboo tongs. Even his calm face was creased with worry. Smiler was such a good-humored baby, you almost never heard him in a temper.

"What's the matter?" Grandma said.

"Smiler can walk," Frankie told her. "Didn't anybody notice?"

Grandma and Grandad came crowding round, patting Smiler on the back, making soft cooing sounds of surprise. Smiler had an explosive fit of hiccups. Grandma Tang dried his tears with a tissue, then his sunny smile came back, proud now, because he was such a clever boy.

"Put him down," Grandma Tang urged Jin, "so he can show us!"

Jin did so and Smiler went toddling off again, like a windup toy, this time toward the massive stone fireplace. Luckily the Tangs never used it to light a fire.

Grandma Tang went scurrying after to stop him falling.

Frankie suddenly realized: "That window is still open."

She reached out to close it, but then they heard a spine-chilling howl coming up from the Oozeburn below. At first, all three of them were stunned into silence. Then Grandad said, "What on earth was that?"

It came again, wild and primitive, but at the same time so melancholy and aching with loneliness that it made Jin shiver.

"Zilombo," he mouthed at Frankie as she slammed the window shut.

And, all at once, Jin, along with his fear, felt real despair. The kind that leaves you feeling sick and hollow inside. As if he'd suddenly realized what they were taking on: what mysterious forces, from ancient times, they were up against. Zilombo was a truly awesome creature. She made the human species seem puny and helpless. No one, not even Mizz Z, knew the limits of her powers.

"What's happened to Mizz Z?" Jin hissed at Frankie.

Then Grandad padded up behind them in his carpet slippers. "Excuse me, children," he said politely.

They both whirled round to look at him. Grandad seemed so serene that you often forgot he had a sharp brain behind that placid face. But now he showed it.

"I believe that something is going on," said Grandad with quiet authority. "And I want you to tell me all about it. And you can tell me too exactly who Mizz Z really is."

Mizz Z was right. The old Zilombo never strayed far from her den. But this Zilombo was much more ambitious. She was a superpredator who felt that the world was her hunting ground. And besides her new physical powers, something else had changed. There were emotions stirring inside her that she'd never felt before.

Zilombo raised a webbed foot, with its wicked claws, to her snout. She sniffed at the red shoelace that she'd tied to her ankle bracelet. Then she whimpered like an abandoned puppy as the Fanta bottle tops softly clinked.

She wanted Smiler back. But did she need him to fill her belly? Or to answer some other need? Even Zilombo herself didn't know that.

She shook her orange Mohawk crest. A hailstorm of tiny shrimps, crabs, and fish scales scattered all around. Under her jutting brow, her piggy eyes gleamed with fury. She snarled and bared her savage teeth. She didn't like those bewildering feelings. She'd like to rip them to pieces, crush them to splinters like bones, so they couldn't bother her any more.

With one great spring, Zilombo leaped from her den entrance. She trotted on all fours along the moonlit towpath to the back door of the factory.

She snuffled at the back doorstep.

She growled as she picked up Smiler's scent.

But she didn't try to kick the back door in. Instead, she gazed upward at those high faraway lights in the Tang's flat and started climbing up the outside of the building.

In Zilombo's den, Mizz Z's body lay crumpled among the fish bones. It seemed lifeless. But suddenly the fingers of one hand twitched. They twitched again. Mizz Z was dreaming—dreaming of the village where she grew up. She saw a fiery sunset flooding the sky with red and purple; she smelled maize cobs, roasting on a barbecue . . .

Suddenly her amber eye shot open.

And Mizz Z realized she wasn't back home. She was in England, in a smelly old sewage pipe. Groggily she tried to work out what had happened. At first her scrambled brain just couldn't make sense of it. But then she remembered the shock, like a bolt of lightning, when she'd lifted Zilombo's hand.

"She electrocuted you!" Mizz Z murmured, half horrified, half impressed.

The old stories said that Zilombo always evolved new skills in her mudball. But this time, it seemed, she'd transformed into a truly formidable creature. And it had all happened on the top of Madalitso's wardrobe in a little gray pebble-dashed bungalow.

Mizz Z tried moving her arms and legs. She was

OK; everything seemed to be in working order.

"You had a very lucky escape," Mizz Z marveled. And it was something she didn't really deserve, because she'd broken her own rules and made a stupid error. "You underestimated Zilombo," she told herself sternly. She'd allowed her personal feelings to cloud her judgment. She, who prided herself on being professional, had gone rushing ahead without thinking. "You are not worthy to be chief inspector of RAAAA!" she added scornfully.

Twenty years ago, singing Zilombo to sleep then cutting her fingernails had been enough to get her back in her mudball. But it wasn't going to be that simple this time. Zilombo had become a deadlier and much more powerful creature. She could shock you if you came anywhere near. She'd even showed flashes of cunning intelligence when she'd tricked Mizz Z into thinking she was asleep. Getting her back in her mudball wasn't going to be easy.

"No more mistakes, A. J. Zauyamakanda!" Mizz Z muttered to herself.

The first thing she needed to do was alert everyone

in the top-floor flat that Zilombo was still on the loose. She crawled on wobbly legs to the pipe entrance. Then she swung across to the ladder and hauled herself up.

The riverbed and the weedy Oozeburn banks trembled with shadows and silvery moonlight. Mizz Z checked to see if Zilombo was lurking anywhere. Surely it would be hard for such a hulking beast to hide herself? Until Mizz Z remembered that Zilombo could now collapse her skeleton and squeeze through the smallest spaces.

"Where are you, Zilombo?" she wondered.

Then she raised her eyes to the factory where the Tangs lived, on the other side of the Oozeburn. There was a huge, dark shape clinging to the front of the building. It moved into a shaft of moonlight and Mizz Z saw a great bull-like head on muscular shoulders, with a crest of orange fur rippling down its spine.

"It's her!" she gasped.

For such a mighty beast, Zilombo was horribly agile. She climbed up the outside of the factory as if it was a cliff face. There were plenty of handholds and footholds on the old Victorian building: ledges and crevices and iron pulleys that had once hoisted sacks up from barges on the river.

Mizz Z staggered back across the iron bridge. She rushed to the back door of the factory. As she ran, she put her hand up to her head. But all she felt was her soft cropped hair.

"Oh no," she breathed. Her head wrap was missing. It must have fallen off in the pipe when she was electrocuted. And it had the back door key tucked into its folds . . .

U p in the Tangs' flat, Jin said, "That's about it."

He, with Frankie chipping in every two seconds, had just finished telling Grandad about Mizz Z and what had hatched from the mudball on top of Madalitso's wardrobe.

Even as he heard himself speaking, Jin thought, *I sound like a crazy person!*

Grandma Tang stood openmouthed and horrified, holding Smiler, who was wriggling to free himself.

But Grandad Tang said, "Have I got this straight? This lady, Mizz Z, visits our city every year. Her job is to inspect ancient artifacts."

"Only the ones that have special powers," Frankie reminded him.

"OK," continued Grandad. "So she makes sure these objects are kept safely, so their ancient powers can't be released and do people harm. But due to circumstances beyond her control, this monstrous beast, this Zilombo, was released from its mudball. And it has made its home in the old sewer pipe on the Oozeburn, just opposite our building."

"Yeah, that's spot-on," nodded Frankie, surprised that their mind-boggling story seemed to make perfect sense to Grandad.

"We thought you'd think we'd gone crazy," added Jin.

But when Grandad was a small boy, sixty years ago in China, he'd heard stories like that all the time. About the mythical beasts and spirits that lived along-side you who walked the village roads, day and night, sometimes invisible, sometimes disguised. Who could even share your house and food.

He'd grown older and moved to another country. But those stories were still part of him. He still knew them all by heart.

"So what do we do?" asked Grandma. "We don't want this horrible creature trying to snatch our Smiler again!" And, as she said this, she hugged Smiler so tightly he yelled in protest.

Suddenly they heard a noise overhead. It wasn't a metro train rattling over the building. This was a different sound. There seemed to be something just above them, scraping and clawing at the tiles like an enormous cat.

Jin stared upward at the ceiling, his skin crawling. *"There's something up there,"* he whispered.

Then Frankie saw something shoot past the window. She went rushing over. Tiles were falling from the roof. There went another one. She gazed after it as it plunged down into murky blackness. Then heard the distant *clink* as it shattered to bits on the Oozeburn towpath.

Down on the towpath, Mizz Z thought, *What's*

going on? as she dodged the falling tiles. Then she realized. *Zilombo's up on the roof!*

Mizz Z's desperation gave her manic strength. She couldn't unlock the back door and it was too solid to break through. So she began to tear the planks off the boarded-up lower windows, trying to get into the factory that way.

Up on the roof, Zilombo thought, *Ugh?* She'd been climbing to reach that bright place where Smiler's howls had come from. But she'd somehow overshot it. She screamed in fury. Her webbed feet drummed the tiles, her ankle bracelet rattled angrily as she crouched astride the roof ridge, silhouetted against the night sky like some enormous gargoyle. Her great beast head seemed to be surrounded by stars.

She threw back her shaggy mane, her muzzle wrinkling as she sniffed the night air.

Her keen wolf scent had detected his smell again. But very faintly. Where was it coming from?

There was a forest of chimney pots up on the roof—old Victorian chimney pots, twisted like candy sticks. Zilombo had no idea what they were. As she rose to her full height to peer down one, they seemed like tunnels, just the kind of dark holes where Smiler might hide. Before her most recent hatching, Zilombo wouldn't have stood a chance of squeezing down there. But now, with her new collapsible skeleton . . .

Rapid wheezing sounds, like a giant wolf panting, came from deep in her belly. Zilombo was sniggering to herself.

She sniffed down one chimney. No, that wasn't where Smiler was hiding. There were many scents rising from the hole, but not his. She tried another chimney. Not that one either. But then a metro train came whooshing overhead, its headlights like the glowing eyes of some monster millipede. Zilombo roared with rage and swiped at it. It rushed away into the dark.

One dozing passenger woke to see a hideous monster trying to derail his train. What on earth was it? It looked like something from a horror movie. "You've just had a terrible nightmare," he tried to reassure himself as the train rushed on.

Meanwhile Zilombo had caught a whiff of Smiler,

drifting across from a different chimney pot.

"Aha!" she croaked triumphantly. She pulled a scaly leg up to her nose to sniff the shoelace on her ankle bracelet. The two smells matched. Headfirst, she began to squeeze herself down the chimney.

CHAPTER
TWELVE

Down in the Tangs' flat, the first sign they were in dreadful danger was when a dead crow fell down the chimney into the fireplace. It was mummified, its feathers all dried up. It had probably been stuck up there for years. Then a cloud of soot burst out into the room. It was Jin who caught on first. While everyone was choking and coughing, he crawled into the fireplace and twisted his head to look upward. As the soot settled, his heart jolted with shock. In the blackness above him, he saw two green eyes, cold as a killer shark's, staring back at him.

Jin scuttled backward out of the fireplace, like a

frightened crab. "It's Zilombo!" he gasped. "She's coming down the chimney!"

There was no time to run. So Grandma Tang crouched down with Smiler behind the sofa. She sat him next to the basket of dragons' eyeballs. "Be a good boy," she hissed. "And play quietly."

A reeking stench of river mud, weeds, and dead crabs came wafting into the room.

"What is that awful smell?" whispered Grandma Tang from behind the sofa.

"Zilombo," hissed Frankie, her eyes fixed on the fireplace.

The first glimpse of the great beast herself was one webbed hand with cruel yellow talons. It slid out of the chimney and scrabbled about on the stone tiles of the hearth.

Then came her sniffing wolf snout, snuffling at the dead crow. No, that wasn't what she wanted. Angrily the clawed hand hurled it away. Its shriveled corpse bounced off the Tangs' white walls and left a black sooty stain.

Then the rest of Zilombo came slithering out. For

a moment, she crouched on the hearthstones while her body swelled again to its usual massive size. Then she shook herself, as a lion shakes off flies. A cloud of soot hid her. But when it settled, Zilombo appeared in her full terrible glory. Her orange mane crested her head and back like a dragon. But her green eyes, under those Neanderthal brows, gleamed with an ancient cunning that seemed horribly human.

Her eyes swiveled in their direction.

"Aha," she croaked, in a voice like a creaky door opening.

Grandma peeked round the sofa; she couldn't help herself. *"Aieee!"* she shrieked. "What is it?"

Downstairs, Mizz Z paused briefly as Grandma Tang's shrill, shocked cry came floating down from the top floor of the factory. Then she renewed her attack on the boarded-up window. She had only one plank to remove before there was a hole big enough for her to climb through. With almost superhuman strength she attacked the wood, ripping out nails, splintering it, not caring how much it tore her hands.

Up in the flat, Zilombo, still crouched on all fours

in the fireplace, began to stamp out a beat on the tiles with one big, flat foot—*boom, boom, boom*, like a war drum. Then, like a kickboxer, her foot shot out sideways. Her ankle bracelet rattled menacingly. Zilombo took a sly, secret look down at her fingers. She made a tiny blue spark dart between them.

"Ugh!" she grunted with satisfaction. Her thin, snake lips curved into a deadly smile.

She couldn't see Smiler yet. But she knew he was close; his smell was very strong. The four puny creatures here would pay for stealing her food store from her. There was no need even to use teeth and claws. She would sizzle them, one after another, like the rat earlier.

No one dared move a muscle. Jin's heart was hammering so hard he thought it would burst through his ribcage. Even Grandad Tang stood stunned with disbelief. He knew all about fantastical mythical beasts. He even made a living out of them. But his dancing dragons were made of paper and fabric. They weren't real, like this flesh and blood, living, breathing monster that crouched in his fireplace. She was so real he could see the golden streaks that flecked her wild, green eyes. And the tiny crabs spilling out of her baggy skin, scuttling away over his carpet.

Then someone broke the spell that had frozen them like ice statues. A sudden crashing din came from behind the sofa.

Smiler had gotten sick of playing with dragons' eyeballs. He'd moved on to the basket of Chinese instruments. Grandma Tang, who'd been staring frozen with fear at Zilombo, suddenly sprang into action. She dived to grab the cymbals off Smiler. But she was too late.

Clash! went the cymbals again.

"Aha!" growled Zilombo, her eyes swiveling toward the sound. She shifted her vast bulk, crouching on her springy legs, getting ready to pounce.

"The dragon!" yelled Grandad Tang desperately. "Jin, dance with me. Frankie, make a big noise! We will chase her away!"

Jin's brain was in a whirling panic. At first, he had no idea what Grandad was talking about. Then he saw Grandad rush over to the two-person dragon propped against the wall. Grandad seized the front bamboo pole and raised the dragon's snarling head high above him, in a shimmer of crimson and gold. But the rest of its body trailed limply on the floor behind him in sad, floppy folds.

Jin knew now what he had to do. He thought crazily, *I can't dragon dance! No way!* But even as this flashed through his mind, he was dashing to pick up the second bamboo pole that supported the dragon's snaky body. He hoisted the pole into the air. Suddenly the dragon came alive, writhing and twisting above him like a great, billowing kite.

Ugh? thought Zilombo, her primitive brain trying to work out what on earth was going on.

The dragon seemed impossible to control. Jin's arms, trying to keep the bamboo pole lifted, were trembling with the effort. Grandad, remembering those old dragon-dancing moves, was swooping the head up and down, so the dragon's eyes rolled and his jaws snapped. Jin knew he should be moving his pole too, making the body dance. But which way?

Up or down, right or left? *I'm going to mess this up!* he thought. And at that precise moment, he was more scared of that than of the monster crouched in the fireplace, baring rows of crocodile fangs.

But then Jin stopped thinking at all. Because Frankie, a stick in her hand, was making her wild, crazy music, bashing away at the drums and gongs. The racket drove all other thoughts from Jin's mind.

Suddenly he found he *could* dragon dance. He didn't have a problem with it at all. He handled that bamboo pole as if he was born to it, following Grandad's lead, making the dragon's body above him rise and dip and swoop like a bird in flight.

For a few seconds, Jin felt ecstatic, taken over completely by the frenzy of the dance. A spirit seemed to lift him out of his own body. He and the dragon became one creature, dancing, flying through the air, graceful and free.

I can do this! he thought, amazed, so happy that tears stung his eyes.

But then the music stopped, abruptly. And Jin and Grandad Tang came slamming back down to earth.

The first thing he saw was Frankie, the stick dangling uselessly by her side. She was staring, petrified. There was no sign of Grandma or Smiler. They were still crouched, hidden, behind the sofa.

Jin turned his head cautiously.

The whole flat was silent, as if time was standing still.

Jin saw Grandad's back right in front of him, and Grandad's raised arms still holding up the dragon's head. Beyond that, he saw Zilombo's scaly chicken legs. Jin felt his heart almost stop. She was really close! She hadn't been chased away. Instead, she'd loped wolflike over to the dragon and risen to her full height. Now she was sniffing his head all over, growling softly.

"Grandad!" hissed Jin. "This isn't working!"

"Wait!" Grandad whispered back. "She has found the mirror."

And then Jin realized. Grandad was pinning all his hopes on the old Chinese story. That Zilombo, like any other dumb beast, wouldn't recognize herself in the mirror. She would think she was looking at a scary monster and run away.

But they should have listened to Mizz Z, who was racing to the rescue, her flip-flops slapping up the stairs: *Never, ever, underestimate Zilombo.*

Mizz Z flung herself into the flat and stood, panting. She saw Zilombo peering into the mirror in the center of the dragon's forehead.

But Zilombo didn't run away, terrified. She backed off a little, surprised. But then she moved closer and peered again.

"Hmmm," said Zilombo, fascinated. She wrinkled her snout. The reflection did the same. She bared her teeth and snarled. So did the reflection. "Aha!" said Zilombo as she suddenly realized. Slowly her snake lips writhed.

"She's smiling at herself in the mirror!" said Mizz Z, aghast. "She knows who she is!"

That meant they were no longer dealing with a dumb beast, with the brain of a dinosaur, or a crocodile. Inside the mudball, Zilombo's brain had evolved, as well as her predator's skills.

She's becoming more human! thought Mizz Z, at

last realizing what Jin had already spotted the first time he'd looked into Zilombo's eyes.

And then Zilombo did something else startling. After she'd recognized her own reflection, she began admiring herself, stroking her Mohawk crest, stiff with river slime, spangled with fish scales. She inspected it from the front, then from the side view. She gave a croak of pleasure, as if she thought she was pretty.

But then Zilombo forgot about the mirror. Because Smiler suddenly wriggled from Grandma Tang's grip. Grandma lunged for him, missed, and Smiler came staggering out from behind the sofa with a big proud grin on his face that said: "Look at me everyone! I'm walking!"

Zilombo's great, shaggy head whipped round. Her tiny green eyes gleamed. She croaked at Smiler, as if in greeting.

Then, before anyone could react, she'd grabbed him.

Frankie was already scrambling over the back of the sofa in a crazy, desperate attempt to get him back.

No way was that monster going to snatch her baby brother again.

"No!" came Mizz Z's urgent warning. "Don't go near her! She'll give you electric shocks!"

"What?" said Frankie, ready to launch herself from the sofa at Zilombo.

"No, Frankie!" yelled Mizz Z again. "She'll kill you!"

Frankie stared in bewilderment at Mizz Z, but she obeyed her and slid back behind the sofa where Gran stood wailing and trembling. "Stop her! Stop her!"

Frankie started hurling gongs, drums. But they bounced off Zilombo's leathery back without her even noticing.

Mizz Z was circling warily around Zilombo, trying to find a way to snatch Smiler back without getting zapped.

Mizz Z crept closer. Zilombo growled at her menacingly and stamped her great flat feet. Her ankle bracelet jangled a warning. She stretched out a webbed hand. Blue sparks jumped between her webbed fingers. Mizz Z skipped back, out of reach.

Grandad reared up the dragon's head again, snapped the fierce teeth, as if to attack. Jin swirled his bamboo pole, to make the body slither like a giant serpent.

But it was no use at all. Zilombo wasn't in the least bit afraid of the Chinese dragon. She had Smiler, a squirming bundle, in the crook of one arm. But with her free hand, she reached out. *Sssst!* Blue sparks shot from her fingertips into the dragon's tufty eyebrows, made of golden wool.

"Fire!" yelled Grandad Tang to Jin as they both threw down their bamboo poles and leaped to a safe distance. The crimson-and-gold dragon went up like a firework in a spectacular *whoosh* of flame and smoke. He burned in seconds to a black skeleton of bamboo hoops.

Grandma Tang screamed again, "Stop the monster!"

But there was nothing anyone could do. Zilombo crashed through the window, with Smiler cradled in her arms, and disappeared into darkness.

As Grandad beat out the last dying embers of the

Chinese dragon, everyone else rushed to the window and gazed out into the night.

Jin looked downward. "Where is she?" he said. He couldn't see Zilombo climbing back down to her Oozeburn den. He thought, horrified, *Perhaps she's fallen!*

But Frankie was staring upward. "There she is! She's climbing up to the roof!"

Grandma Tang was in hysterics. "Get my Smiler back!" she was shrieking, over and over again. "My poor baby. This is a nightmare!"

Jin put his arm round her shaking shoulders to comfort her. "I don't think she'll hurt him," he found himself saying.

Jin had peeped from under the dragon. When Zilombo had first seen Smiler, *he'd* been watching *her*. And with his great skill at reading faces, Jin had noticed something. He'd noticed Zilombo's savage features softening. And something a bit like love creeping over her face.

Jin told Grandma, "Maybe she likes Smiler." It sounded crazy, even to him.

And Grandma Tang definitely thought he was off his rocker. "What are you talking about?" she screamed at him. "You saw her! She's a brute, a monster!"

Only Mizz Z didn't seem surprised. She, too, had seen human feelings in Zilombo's face. But that didn't mean she trusted Zilombo not to follow her beastly instincts. That she'd captured Smiler alive, hadn't instantly zapped him, didn't mean anything at all. Zilombo liked her food to be fresh and wriggling.

That little nerve began pulsing just below Mizz Z's eye patch, like a tiny heartbeat. She had to fight to stop memories overwhelming her. But when she spoke, it was in her brisk, superconfident chief inspector's voice.

"Don't worry," Mizz Z told Grandma Tang. "You will have your Smiler back before you know it. Now, how do we get out onto the roof? Is there a trap door?"

CHAPTER

THIRTEEN

Zilombo climbed quickly. She had both hands free because she held Smiler in her teeth, by the back of his overalls.

Smiler was puzzled. But he wasn't terrified. After all, he'd met Zilombo before. And he was too little to know that in human terms she was a monster—that bigger kids would run screaming from her in horror. Besides that, his baby brain knew instinctively that Zilombo didn't mean, at that precise moment, to hurt him. She'd cradled him in her arms. Now she held him with her teeth. But her grip was gentle, like a mother crocodile carrying her babies tenderly from place to place in her jaws.

179

Zilombo reached the roof. But then she climbed higher. She swung herself like a great ape through the girders, to the metro bridge that ran above the factory.

She put Smiler next to the rails, then squatted down beside him.

The night breeze ruffled her orange mane. From here she could see her whole territory, all the city lights twinkling. This new Zilombo wasn't content anymore with small, dark dens. She wanted much more power than that.

"Hmmm," she grunted in satisfaction. She felt like Queen of the World, like everything she could see from here, the city and the river running through it, was hers.

And now she had Smiler to keep her from being lonely. She searched in the folds of her skin and, in a friendly way, passed him a tiny red crab to munch.

"Goo," Smiler thanked her. Fascinated, he watched the crab scuttle over his fingers.

Monster and baby sat for a moment, side by side, in silence.

Smiler gazed about him, entranced, his eyes wide

with wonder. He'd never been in such a magical place. Smiler loved shiny things, and up here he didn't know where to look first. There was the city below him, sparkling like a million lit-up Christmas trees, and overhead the twinkling stars and the giant silver bauble of the moon.

"Ahhh," said Smiler, trying to reach up to grab it.

He was so bewitched that he didn't hear the rumbling from Zilombo's belly. The great beast had remembered she was hungry. Her belly rumbled again. It was a while since she'd crunched that fried rat. And there was nothing up here to eat.

Yes, there was. Her eyes took on a predator's gleam. They slid craftily sideways to spy at Smiler. She just couldn't help herself. Hunger pangs griped in her belly. Her muzzle dripped saliva.

Before, she wouldn't have thought twice about it. She'd have seen him as nothing but prey, to scoff immediately or to put in her food store.

But now there was a struggle going on inside her.

She didn't want to eat him. Yes, she did. No, she didn't. Yes, she did.

She fought desperately against those primitive

predator's instincts that had always ruled her. But they were too powerful. The stabbing talons on her great monster's paw twitched, reached out . . .

Then Smiler, still trying to catch the moon, missed and his slimy hand patted Zilombo's snout. In return Zilombo licked his face with her rough, furry tongue. She began searching his spiky hair for fleas like a gorilla mum would do.

She wasn't going to eat Smiler. She needed him to fill the great aching hole in her heart, not her belly.

But then Zilombo's empty belly gave an extra savage gripe. Those hunger pangs really hurt her. She moaned softly and rocked to and fro. She bent down her shaggy head. She meant to lick Smiler's face affectionately but instead, she caught a whiff of his scent. *Mmmm*, she thought as she licked his face greedily.

Then her guts gave another painful twist. Zilombo's snake lips writhed, they pulled back from those crocodile teeth. Saliva dripped from her jaws onto his hair. And quite suddenly, any tender feelings she'd had for the human child were whisked clean out of her head.

She was predator again, pure and simple. And Smiler was just an easy way of filling her belly. She didn't even have to chase him—he was already in her grasp.

But just as her claws closed around Smiler, Zilombo heard something. What was it? Zilombo's great beast's head slowly turned. Then it came again: a faint clatter in the distance—a challenge, like the warlike clash of her own ankle bracelet.

She gazed out over the city skyline, head lifted, muzzle sniffing the air.

Then the rails by her big, flat feet started to hum with a weird metallic song.

Something was coming this way. Something big, speeding toward her, fast as a cheetah.

"Ugh?"

Connections were being made, slowly, in Zilombo's brain. It was the creature she'd seen before, trying to muscle in on her territory, take her place as top predator. And, more than that, it was going to steal her dinner.

Zilombo felt fury sweep through her like a raging torrent. With the back of her hand, she cuffed Smiler away from the tracks. She didn't want him damaged in the coming fight. She liked her prey fresh and alive.

Then she rose to her full height, threw back her massive head and roared out a challenge that echoed over the city.

The metro train came swaying and rattling above the rooftops, its headlamps like fierce, glowing eyes. It was still far away. But Zilombo didn't wait for it to arrive. She ran to meet it, with mighty bounds, springing along beside the track.

The shocked driver blasted his horn. Zilombo roared back. Then she attacked.

She hurled herself at the train's shiny sides, her claws gouging and tearing its metal skin, blue sparks flying from her fingers as she tried to shock it. But it was a fight that even the mighty Zilombo couldn't win. Metro trains were grounded against electricity. Her claws ripped the metal to shreds but couldn't stop the train. As it raced toward the factory with Zilombo clinging to the roof like a giant starfish, it rocked suddenly round a curve. Zilombo found herself slipping. She fought to hold on but she slid down the carriage sides, her dragging nails leaving ten long scratches. Then the train swayed again and she was flung off, still roaring and slashing, perilously close to the track.

She tried to roll clear but didn't quite make it. The wheels of the last carriage sped over her long talons and severed her fingernails, like a circular saw. The train clattered over the factory and the posh hotel and sped away into darkness, its glowing windows like shooting stars.

Zilombo got up dizzily, growling in fury. She wanted to attack again. She started chasing after the train, trying to run it down as she'd run down so much prey in the past.

But already her power was draining, her muscles weakening. Her sprint turned to a stagger. She gave up the chase, spun round, and tried to find Smiler. Maybe fresh meat would revive her strength. But she couldn't even do that; her sight was dimming. Everything seemed hazy, like the mist that creeps over a lake before dawn.

Using the last of her strength, she climbed on top of the bridge parapet.

Mizz Z, the Tangs, and Jin and Frankie were clustered on the factory roof below. They were gazing up, horrified. They'd arrived just in time to see Zilombo's doomed battle with the metro train.

They watched as she stood there swaying, disoriented, her grotesque shape silhouetted against the moon.

Jin's heart was clenched in panic: "Has she got Smiler?"

"No," said Mizz Z. "She's all alone."

Then Zilombo pitched off the bridge and began falling. She tumbled through space, her orange mane making a fiery halo around her.

They all rushed to the edge of the factory roof, looked over.

"She's falling toward the Oozeburn," said Jin.

But it was like a dark pit down there. They couldn't see where she landed.

"Good," announced Grandad Tang, his kindly voice more steely and merciless than Jin had ever heard it. "Even *she* couldn't survive that fall."

And then no one was thinking about Zilombo anymore, because from the metro bridge above them came a thin, distant wail.

"It's Smiler!" cried Grandma Tang. "Are you all right, my precious boy?"

A shaky "Goo!" came drifting down. Now that Zilombo was gone, Smiler was feeling alone and abandoned, up there among the stars.

Mizz Z shouted up instructions to him: "Stay there, Smiler! Do not move one millimeter!"

"He's too little to understand!" gabbled Jin frantically. Mizz Z knew an awful lot, about a great many things. But she didn't have a clue about babies.

"Hang on, Bro!" yelled Frankie, hitching up her black flouncy skirts and heading toward the girders. "I'm coming up there to get you!"

CHAPTER FOURTEEN

Mizz Z dragged Frankie back. "You are not going up there," she said, flashing her eye at her. "It's my job. I am chief inspector."

"You can't tell me what to do! You're not my mum!" said Frankie, tearing away and scrambling up the girders, out of reach.

"That girl," said Mizz Z, shaking her head and tutting. "She is so headstrong. She reminds me of me when I was her age."

"Smiler might fall!" wailed Grandma Tang, wringing her hands. She was clutching Bobo, Smiler's favorite toy. The tatty monkey was already soaked with her tears. "A metro train might run him over!"

"Don't worry," said Mizz Z, planting a flip-flop on the first girder. "We are going to get your grandson. How long between trains?"

"About half an hour," said Grandad.

"Take Bobo," said Grandma, thrusting the soggy, battered chimp at Mizz Z.

"Sorry," said Mizz Z briskly. "Have to leave him down here. I need both hands free to climb." Then she paused, and kicked off her shoes. "I'd be better off climbing without these too," she said.

Jin watched as his sister and Mizz Z climbed the crisscross framework of iron girders to the metro bridge above. He thought briefly of joining them.

Then he warned himself, "Jin, don't push your luck!"

Since Mizz Z had exploded into Jin's life like a multicolored rocket, he'd done amazing things. Things he'd never dreamed he was capable of. Like rescuing Smiler from the sewer pipe. Then dragon dancing with Grandad. But Jin knew his limits. He couldn't make that climb. So he stayed where he was on the factory roof, gazing upward, feeling sick with anxiety.

"Come down, Frankie," cried Grandma Tang. "You'll fall."

"She won't fall, Grandma," Jin tried to comfort her. "She climbs all over the place to spray her tag."

But, Jin guessed, Frankie had never made this particular climb before: even she had thought it was too risky. You could see that metro bridge from his grandparents' flat. And Jin had never noticed any red dragons sprayed there. There was no graffiti on it at all.

Frankie and Mizz Z were a long way up now, almost at the bridge. They looked like two giant insects—a bright tropical butterfly and a black moth—that had landed on those rusty iron girders.

"Stay still, Smiler, stay still until they reach you," murmured Grandad, his fists clenched so hard the knuckles were white as bone.

"She should have taken Bobo," wailed Grandma. "To comfort my poor little boy."

Listening to his distraught grandparents, Jin had one of those odd, random thoughts he often had when things got deadly serious: *Wonder if that metal is hurting Mizz Z's bare feet?*

But if the metal hurt her, Mizz Z didn't show it. She soon caught up with Frankie. Then suddenly Frankie stopped climbing. She clung to the girders, her arms wrapped tightly around them. The night breeze whipped her hair and moaned in the metal. Frankie's teeth started chattering. She felt icy cold. She just couldn't move, couldn't go up, or down.

"I-I'm going to fall," stammered Frankie, forcing the words through frozen lips. The last few hours had been surreal and deeply scary. Smiler had been kidnapped not once, but twice, by a terrifying monster. The stress and craziness of it all had finally caught up with Frankie.

But then came Mizz Z's voice, right by her ear, as calm as if they were taking a stroll in the park. "No, you are *not* going to fall," Mizz Z contradicted Frankie, as if the idea was ridiculous. "Trust me when I say it! Do you trust me?"

Frankie, hugging the girders even more desperately, turned her head, to meet that steady amber gaze.

"Yes, I trust you," she heard herself saying. Which made the day's events even more surprising. Because Frankie didn't give her trust easily.

"Then let's get moving," said Mizz Z. "We are almost there." She sounded casual but she was thinking about that next metro train.

Mizz Z climbed the bridge parapet first, then reached down and hauled Frankie after her.

"Smiler!" said Frankie, her moment of paralyzing panic forgotten.

Smiler was sitting huddled against the bridge parapet, a small, lost, bewildered baby. But when he saw Frankie, he gave her a great drooling grin. She went running up.

"Do not walk on the rails!" Mizz Z reminded her. "One of them will be live. It will shock you, as sure as Zilombo."

Frankie snatched Smiler up, hugging him as if she'd never let him go. Then she cried, "Mizz Z! Look at this!"

Lying scattered by the metro rail were ten long yellow talons, neatly severed.

"So that is the reason Zilombo fell," murmured Mizz Z to herself. "I was wondering why."

"What?" said Frankie. "What did you say?"

Mizz Z shook herself, seemed to come out of a dream. Was that a metro train rattling in the distance? She said in her brisk chief inspector's voice, "We must get this baby safely down to the factory roof. Do you have any spare material in that dress?"

"*Errr*, yes, loads," said Frankie, glancing down at all the layers, frills, and flounces of her, by now, very tatty-looking party frock.

"Then tear some off," said Mizz Z.

Frankie put Smiler down again and ripped off a few frills.

Deftly Mizz Z tied them into a sling, then tested it for strength. "Hmmm, that will do," she said. She picked up Smiler and put him into the sling. She swung him onto her back, then tied the sling across her chest. "Right, let us go," Mizz Z said. She gave a searching look to Frankie. "Are you OK?"

"Yep," nodded Frankie. "I'm OK."

"Then I will go first," said Mizz Z. With Smiler on

her back, she lowered herself over the parapet, feeling for footholds on the girders with her bare feet.

Smiler had stopped squirming. He had his head resting on Mizz Z's back. He could hear her heartbeat. And suddenly he didn't even need Bobo to get to sleep. Mizz Z's heartbeat soothed him. His eyelids drooped; his legs, sticking out of the sling, went floppy. Smiler was in the land of dreams.

Frankie was about to climb back over the parapet. She took one last glance around her, at the empty rail line soaring off into darkness. At the city below her, still humming with traffic and twinkling with lights. At the moon and stars above. It was like being on top of the world. She took a great lungful of cool night air to steady her nerves for the climb down.

She knew she'd probably never come up here again. On impulse, she took her spray can out of her secret pocket. This was the highest point she'd ever climbed to. She wanted to leave some reminder. Something that told everyone: "Frankie was here!"

She leaned over the parapet and sprayed her Chinese dragon defiantly on the outside of the parapet, her personal signature, up here for all to see.

A voice came from below. It was Mizz Z, in her most disapproving tones. "You should not do that!" she called. "That is illegal!"

Frankie grinned. "Yeah, yeah, Mizz Z," she murmured.

She was about to stash the spray can in her pocket and follow Mizz Z down to the factory roof. But somehow she fumbled it and the spray can slipped from her fingers. She grabbed for it and missed. Her precious can clanged once off the girders then, like Zilombo, it went spinning down through space and was lost in the dark pit of the Oozeburn.

Frankie cursed. She felt irritation flash through her. That can had been a bargain, much bigger than the tiny paint cans she could usually afford.

But suddenly she shrugged. "It's not a big deal, Frankie," she told herself. What did one spray can matter, when they'd just rescued Smiler from a monster's clutches?

"What are you doing up there?" Mizz Z's call came

floating up from below. "The next metro will be along any minute!"

"I'm coming right now, Mizz Z!" Frankie called back and, grinning even more broadly, she began to climb downward.

On the factory roof, Jin watched Mizz Z descending, with Smiler strapped to her back. He felt wild relief that Smiler was safe. But there was another feeling too—as he watched the heroic rescue, he'd stood fidgeting beside Grandma and Grandad. He felt useless. *I'm down here with the old people!* he fretted. He desperately wanted to be part of the action.

Grandma Tang couldn't wait to see Smiler. "Is the poor baby all right?" she called up to Mizz Z.

"Yes, he is fine," Mizz Z called back. "And Zilombo is no danger now! Her fingernails have been sliced off. Thank goodness for her Achilles heel!"

"Fingernails and Achilles heel?" echoed Grandad Tang, baffled. "What's she talking about?"

But Jin knew. He'd been full of doubts when Grandad said, "Surely even *she* couldn't survive that fall!" Because hadn't Mizz Z always warned them?

"Never, ever, underestimate Zilombo." But now he knew about her sliced-off nails, Jin was sure the monster had finally been defeated. If the fall hadn't killed her, she'd have shrunk up inside her mudball. Just like she'd done when Mizz Z's dad cut her nails. Even the formidable Zilombo was harmless in there. She couldn't hurt anyone now.

Jin felt happiness surge through him. It was brilliant news. But almost as good as that, he knew exactly what to do next. At last he could play a part.

"I'm off down to the Oozeburn," he told Gran and Grandad Tang. "To find the mudball."

Gran and Grandad didn't reply. They were too busy gazing upward, hearts in mouths, watching Mizz Z and Frankie climb down.

So Jin slipped quietly away, unnoticed.

CHAPTER
FIFTEEN

Jin strolled in the moonlight along the Oozeburn's weedy towpath, peering under bramble bushes, searching through the long grass. He felt quite relaxed. He was thinking how pleased Mizz Z would be if he found the mudball. What would she do with it? Would it go back on top of Madalitso's wardrobe?

He was even humming happily to himself at how well things had turned out, against all the odds. But, wait. What was that sound? He stopped in mid step. *Rattle, rattle.* There it went again. Jin's whole body froze with shock. "No, it can't be!" he whispered.

But then it sounded for a third time, that tinny

jangling noise he knew so well. His skin instantly started crawling.

"Zilombo?" he shuddered, still not quite believing. It couldn't be her. If she was alive, she'd be shut up in her mudball now, no danger to anyone.

Jin was now opposite her den in the old sewer pipe. He gazed across into its shadowy entrance. The grid was back in place, which made it hard to see inside.

"There's nothing there," Jin convinced himself. A great wave of relief crashed through him. "You just imagined it!"

He was about to carry on looking for the mudball when his heart chilled again. Was that a flash of orange behind the grid? Filled with dread, Jin peered again. But in the tangle of moonlight and shadows, he just couldn't be certain.

Then, with a massive *crash*, the grid exploded out of the pipe. A shaft of moonlight shone on the pipe entrance, lighting up the inside. And this time there was no mistake.

"It's her!" Jin gasped as an orange Mohawk crest

and a snarling muzzle poked out of the pipe. "She's alive!"

Quickly Jin dived into the long grass. For a few seconds there was silence. His heart hammering, Jin parted the grass stems carefully to peer through.

He saw her squatting in the den entrance. How had she survived that fall? But not only that—her fingernails had grown again! Those yellow, stabbing talons were even longer, sharper than before.

What's going on? he thought, his mind a whirl of panic and confusion. Didn't Mizz Z say Zilombo always shut herself up in a mudball to grow new fingernails? Didn't it sometimes take years, even centuries, for her to hatch out again?

But Mizz Z had also said, "Never, *ever*, underestimate Zilombo." When Smiler drooled on her mudball Zilombo had hatched with new powers—the collapsing skeleton, the stingray shocks. And this was another one no one knew about. She could regenerate missing body parts in double-quick time, just like starfish grow new arms, lizards new tails.

A sound like a heron's squawk came from her throat. Zilombo was laughing. Just to amuse herself some more she made electric sparks shoot between her fingers. "Aha!" she croaked, holding up her blue, sizzling paws.

"She's indestructible," whispered Jin, shuddering.

Then suddenly he kicked something with his trainer. It gave a soft *clunk*. Jin swiveled his head round. It was the spray can that Frankie had dropped from the metro bridge. He grabbed it so it didn't clunk again.

But Zilombo heard the noise. Her swivel eyes turned and scanned the towpath. She snarled, showing bone-crunching teeth.

Jin stopped peeking, ducked his head lower, and tried to stay very still.

Meanwhile, up on the factory roof, Mizz Z and Frankie had climbed down to safety. Mizz Z unslung Smiler from her back and put him in Grandma Tang's arms.

He woke up and cried a bit but Grandma Tang gave him Bobo to cuddle and he went back to sleep again.

"Thank you," said Grandma Tang, all smiles now

that Smiler was safe. She bowed low to Mizz Z. "Thank you, thank you," she said again.

Mizz Z bowed deeply back. "I was only doing my job as chief inspector."

Then suddenly Frankie looked round. "Where's Jin?" she demanded.

Grandma and Grandad were still cooing over Smiler. They didn't seem to have heard.

"Perhaps you could tell us where he's gone?" said Mizz Z more politely.

"He went down to the Oozeburn," Grandad told her. "He said something about looking for the mudball. Oh dear," said Grandad, suddenly sounding worried, "do you think I should have stopped him?"

Mizz Z was already striding toward the trap door. She shot a sharp glance at Frankie. Frankie hurried to join her. She could tell, from Mizz Z's face, that she was having grim thoughts.

"You don't think it's over, do you?" Frankie said, with dawning horror. "You think she might still be alive!"

"Never, *ever* . . ." began Mizz Z.

". . . underestimate Zilombo," finished Frankie as they both sprinted toward the stairs.

Down on the Oozeburn's banks, Jin lay hidden, clutching Frankie's spray can.

He still wasn't sure if Zilombo had seen him. Maybe he could escape and warn the others. He had to know what she was doing. Holding his breath, he parted the grass stems once again and made himself a tiny spy hole.

The great beast had turned her back. She'd retreated into her den, perhaps to zap a sewer rat for a crispy snack.

Jin breathed again. Good, that meant she hadn't seen him yet. But he couldn't stay here. "You've got to warn the others she's alive," he told himself. Mizz Z would know what to do. It was only a few meters to the factory. He could drag himself commando-style through the weeds. Then slip in the same way he'd gotten out, through the ground-floor windows where Mizz Z had ripped off the boards.

But he hadn't counted on Zilombo's wolflike

hearing. He'd barely started to crawl when she heard the grasses rustle. Her head whipped round. Something big was out there. She croaked excitedly, springing to the mouth of her den. It was about time she had some proper food, meat to gnaw, bones to crack.

And this time she saw exactly where he was. She roared—a savage blood-curdling howl of triumph, foam dripping from her jaws.

Jin froze.

Zilombo roared again and stamped her feet. Her ankle bracelet rattled furiously.

"She's seen me!" thought Jin. He panicked and leaped up, meaning to run. But then Zilombo fixed him with her tiny, killer shark eyes. And Jin knew he had no chance.

His fingers tightened in terror around Frankie's spray can. Then, without thinking, he just threw it.

Zilombo's swivel eyes followed it as it flew toward her. She was a mighty mythical beast, a creature older than dinosaurs. But she'd never seen a spray can before. She caught it with her paw.

"Ugh?" she croaked to herself.

Was this thing alive? Was it like a crab, in a shell with delicious meat inside? She turned it round and round in her talons.

Jin tried to stop himself trembling, to stand perfectly still. She seemed to have forgotten him. But Jin knew she hadn't. She still had one swivel eye on him. If he tried to run, she'd use those powerful legs. She'd launch herself out of that den and leap across the canal in one spring like a giant velociraptor.

Zilombo brought the can up to her nose to sniff, prodded it with her claws.

Suddenly it sprayed in her face, just like a squid or cuttlefish sprays ink at its enemies. Zilombo hurled it away, roaring with anger. It rolled farther into the pipe. On all fours, she chased after it. It was getting away! Furiously she gave it a double blast of her latest weapon. Like two lightning bolts, electricity flashed from both her hands.

KA-BOOM! The massive explosion deep inside the pipe rocked the ground like an earthquake.

Mizz Z and Frankie, who were rushing toward the den, were hurled to the towpath. They covered their heads as mud and stones rained down. Slowly the shock waves died away. Frankie lay there, stunned, her ears ringing.

"Wha-what happened?" she stuttered as Mizz Z hauled her to her feet.

But Mizz Z was already shouting: "Jin, Jin, where are you?" Her eye peered along the bank, through the moonlight and shadows. After the big, underground explosion, an eerie hush had settled on the Oozeburn. Nothing moved or made a sound.

"Jin!" shouted Mizz Z more urgently. "Speak to me!"

There was no answer.

Then, just along the bank, some tall grasses shook. They shook again. A figure staggered out, wobbly on its feet, muddy and scratched by bramble bushes.

"I think I'm OK," Jin called out in a shaky voice.

They both went running toward him. His sister gave him a joyful high five: "Hey, Bro!"

Frankie's head had finally stopped buzzing. She stared at the few wisps of smoke curling out of the mouth of Zilombo's den. "What happened?" she asked again.

Jin said, "Well, Zilombo wasn't in her mudball like we thought. She was still alive!"

Mizz Z nodded sagely. "I wondered if she might be."

"Anyhoo," said Jin, "I found the spray can Frankie dropped and I chucked it into her den and she zapped it with electricity and—"

"It exploded like a bomb," Frankie finished the sentence for him. "That's why dad hates me keeping those cans under my bed. You ever read the warnings on them? It says stuff like: EXTREMELY FLAMMABLE! DO NOT IGNITE! WILL EXPLODE IN CONFINED SPACES!"

"You threw the can into her den?" Mizz Z asked Jin. "That was a very brave thing to do."

Jin shuffled about, embarrassed. "I just chucked it without thinking," he tried to explain. His aim was usually so bad that he was amazed now that the can had gone anywhere near its target. And he hadn't even remembered that it could explode.

But Mizz Z wouldn't be contradicted. "Nevertheless, you are quite a hero!" she insisted.

Jin couldn't believe his ears. He'd been called *wise* and *hero*, all in one day!

He still shrugged modestly and said, "Naaah, it was nothing." But he stored the word *hero* away in his mind, where it sparkled like a precious jewel. And he thought secretly, *Maybe I am!*

"So is Zilombo finally dead?" asked Frankie.

"Wait here," said Mizz Z. She crossed the iron bridge to the other side of the Oozeburn. She couldn't climb down the iron ladder because it was too hot to touch. So she stared down into the entrance of what had once been Zilombo's den. There was a terrible smell of burning. The sewer pipe was scorched black; it must have collapsed inside. The den was full of smoking rocks and tangled metal that still glowed red-hot. Nothing, not even Zilombo, could have survived that.

"Yes," nodded Mizz Z. "This time she's really dead."

"Good riddance!" rejoiced Frankie.

But Jin's feelings were more mixed. It was Jin, after all, with his ace face-reading skills, who had glimpsed flashes of human feeling in Zilombo's face.

And Mizz Z was feeling sorry too. "At least she felt no pain," she said. "Death must have been instant."

Jin muttered, "And I thought she was indestructible." And suddenly he had doubts. He called to Mizz Z, "You sure she's dead?"

Mizz Z frowned. Was she uncertain too? But then she stooped to pick something up from among the burnt weeds on the Oozeburn bank. At first, Jin couldn't make out what the blackened object was that dangled from Mizz Z's hand.

Then, with a shiver, he recognized it. It was Zilombo's bottle-top ankle bracelet that she'd stolen from Mizz Z's brother Kapito when she'd captured him. It must have been blown off in the blast.

"Zilombo would never take this off," declared Mizz Z in a solemn voice. "In my opinion, this means she is dead, without any doubt." She hesitated for a moment. The ankle bracelet still dangled from her hand, as if she didn't know what to do with it.

Frankie called a suggestion across the Ooozeburn.

"Why don't you give it back to Kapito?"

Mizz Z thought about this. Then she shook her head. "No, I don't think so," she decided. "Kapito is grown up now. He is a young man. He doesn't want to remember that bad time in the past. And neither do I." Suddenly she threw the bracelet away. It flew clinking through the air and landed in the mud of the Oozeburn, where it vanished, sucked down without a trace.

Mizz Z came striding back over the bridge.

"Zilombo's history now," said Frankie.

But Mizz Z said, with something like regret in her voice, "She was a magnificent creature. Truly unique." And she stood for a moment in silence, head bowed, honoring Zilombo. Then, with one last heavy sigh, she raised her head.

When she spoke again, her voice was brisk and businesslike, just like a chief inspector's should be. "I must go now," she told Jin and Frankie as she retrieved her bangles from the bramble bush.

Jin's mouth just hung open. Frankie said, shocked, "What, so soon?"

"Unfortunately, yes," said Mizz Z. "I must get the first flight out of here. They will be expecting me at RAAAA HQ. They will want my report on the Zilombo affair ASAP. I shall just collect my laptop."

And then she was gone, back into the factory.

Jin and Frankie heard her flip-flops slapping as she strode up the stairs to Grandma and Grandad Tang's flat.

They stared at each other, stunned.

"I can't believe she's going," said Frankie, shaking her head in disbelief. "I thought she might hang around, at least for a few days."

"Come on," said Jin, at last springing into action. "We can't let her go without saying goodbye."

They raced into the building. Grandma Tang was standing by the front door, still clutching Smiler in her arms. He was still fast asleep.

"Your grandad is giving Mizz Z a lift to the airport," she told them. "She wanted to call a taxi but we wouldn't hear of it!"

Jin and Frankie ran outside. But Grandad's four-wheel drive was just pulling off. They could see Mizz

Z in the passenger seat beside him.

"We're too late!" said Jin, crushed by disappointment.

But the window slid down and Mizz Z poked out her head. She waved at Jin and Frankie. *"Tionana!"* she shouted. Then the window slid down again and the four-wheel drive made a left turn and disappeared.

"Tionana, what's that mean?" said Frankie.

Jin said, "It's probably Chewa. I bet it means goodbye." He frowned unhappily. He just couldn't believe that Mizz Z had vanished from his life, as quickly as she'd come into it. Not after all they'd been through together.

"Think we'll ever see her again?" asked Frankie.

"I don't know," said Jin. "Maybe not."

"I'm going to miss her," Frankie suddenly declared.

"Me too."

The next day, back at home, Jin was sitting in his bedroom, playing a computer game. He was zapping zombies. But he was doing it automatically, without thinking. What he was *actually* thinking was: *Wonder how the Lakeside Queens are doing in the schoolgirls' football league?*

Suddenly Frankie came crashing into his bedroom. "Hi, Bro!"

"You should knock before you come in," said Jin without turning round. "Anyway, where have you been?" he asked her.

"I've been down to the shops for Mum."

"Have you and Mum made it up?" asked Jin.

"Course," said Frankie impatiently. "We always do, don't we? But I don't want to talk about that. I've been looking something up on the net."

"What?" said Jin, not very interested, zapping another zombie.

"You know that word Mizz Z said as she was leaving?"

"Yeah, *tionana* or something?" said Jin, feeling rather more interested.

"Well, it doesn't mean what you thought."

Jin turned round and stared at Frankie. Now he was *really* paying attention.

"You know how you thought it meant goodbye?" said Frankie.

"What else could it mean?" asked Jin.

"Well, it doesn't actually mean goodbye. It means something more like, 'I will return.'"

"I will return?" repeated Jin, puzzled. There was a pause. Then the full meaning of Frankie's news finally hit him. "Hey, that means we'll see her again!"

"*Doh!* Yes, it does!" said Frankie, shaking her head in amazement that Jin had taken so long to understand the good news. "It means that Mizz Z is *definitely* coming back!"

EPILOGUE

Madalitso recovered and came out of the hospital.

Grandma and Grandad Tang moved out of the factory and found bigger and better premises to rent for their Chinese dragon business.

The Lakeside Queens won the schoolgirls' football league.

And Zilombo?

Even Mizz Z thought the mighty monster must be dead. And Zilombo *was* terribly damaged in the blast. She lost one of her scaly chicken legs and one of her beast paws. But her collapsible skeleton saved her. She wriggled through smoking wreckage into a narrow crack in the mud bank. There she encased herself in her mudball to recover. But could even the great Zilombo survive such injuries? Probably not. Except, inside the mudball she'd evolved a new power. She could grow herself new limbs, to replace missing ones, like a starfish does.

When she discovered this, anyone passing on the banks of the Oozeburn would have heard a strange sound from deep underground.

It was the sound of Zilombo, laughing.